BOOK ONE OF THE MOVEMENT TRILOGY

THE
SETTLERS

JASON GURLEY

The Settlers

Jason Gurley

Copyright © 2013 Jason Gurley
www.jasongurley.com

Cover art copyright © Greg Martin
www.artofgregmartin.com

The Movement Trilogy

The Settlers

The Colonists

Other Novels

Greatfall

The Man Who Ended the World

For Felicia and Emma
Who better to spend this one life with

ASYLUM

The first settlers were empty-handed.

They walked up the street like nomads. Fathers with arms around their wives. Children holding hands, their expressions bleak. The old people followed, pushing their walkers through ankle-deep water. They would be turned back long before they reached the spaceport. But still they followed.

They were survivors already, cast from ruined homes by a tempestuous planet. Their neighborhoods were underwater, or would soon be. The trees they had planted as children were uprooted, and floated like barges through the streets and canals. They had watched their loved ones die, often just beyond their reach.

The first settlers were in a collective state of shock.

Tasneem Kyoh was five years old then. Later she would struggle to remember life before that gray, damp morning. Surely she had formed memories of play dates, of birthdays, of watching cartoons on Saturday mornings -- but as an adult, she could not recall a single one.

It was as if her life began at the moment Earth died.

And after that day, she remembers everything.

Nobody knew it would happen so quickly.

For decades, environmentalists and scientists had warned that Earth had a tipping point, an invisible line that, when crossed, would bring irreversible change. Temperatures and sea levels would become unpredictable. Weather systems previously unheard of would surge into historically calm regions.

Only a few listened.

Change was too distant. It was too surreal. Filmmakers made movies about the disasters to come, but these failed as warnings. The content of the films were fantastic, unreal. Who could relate to the state of Colorado cracking in half? Almost nobody. And so, as politicians downplayed the crisis, the coming change became a fiction. A fairy tale.

And for years, it seemed that maybe the scientists had been wrong.

Oh, there were moments: great hurricanes that took unpredictable turns and landed on the wrong coasts. Coastal erosion that took entire resort communities down into the sea almost instantly. Winter storms that threatened traditionally warm climates.

It was hard to string isolated moments together into a warning.

But the great ice sheets at both poles collapsed and

vanished, and suddenly more cities were built on waterways. These new cities collided with land, were swallowed up by immense waves. Temperatures rose, and the storms attacked mercilessly. The Earth turned on itself.

Humanity just happened to be in the way.

The years that followed challenged mankind in ways it had never imagined. While people all over the planet were submitted to terrible storms and watched their homes destroyed, rebuilt and destroyed again, world governments worked together to construct man's failsafe: a great home in space, where millions would be able to live free of the daily fear of death and loss.

It took thirty-three years to build the first space station.

In ordinary circumstances, such an undertaking should have been carefully planned and spread over half a century or more. To the average human, however, one who lived in abject fear of abrupt and horrible death, thirty-three years might as well have been ten thousand.

When construction began in 2047, the world's population was nine billion, down from 10.5 billion just three years before. The Earth's unstable season claimed lives in startling numbers, with incredible speed. When Station Ganymede was brought online in 2080, Earth's population was just 4.2 billion.

The new space station would provide a home for 3 million people.

Ganymede was humanity's greatest achievement, and it was only a life preserver.

Man was weakening.

Jason Gurley

TASNEEM

TREATMENT

Name?

Tasneem.

Last name?

Kyoh.

The nurse looks up at Tasneem, then back down at her documents. Birthplace?

Seattle, Washington.

Age?

Thirty-three.

Birthdate?

June 11, 2075.

The nurse records this, then asks, Do you currently take any medications, or have any conditions that are under treatment?

No, ma'am.

History of cancer in your immediate family?

Tasneem nods. My father. Lung cancer.

What year?

I'm sorry?

What year did your father pass?

Oh. Right. 2068.

The nurse nods. The cloudburst, yes?

Yes. Did you lose anyone?

Eleven in my family, the nurse says. She shakes her head. Can you believe that? Just like that.

I remember.

The nurse clucks her tongue. It was a dark time. How about heart disease?

Tasneem struggles to keep up with the nurse's change of topic. No. Not that I know of.

Okay. Heart disease, no. Sexual activity?

Tasneem shakes her head. I -- I haven't.

The nurse glances up again, squints at Tasneem. Do you mean ever, or recently?

I haven't, Tasneem repeats. Ever.

No sexual activity, the nurse says to herself, making a note on Tasneem's file.

Thirty-three years old, and still she is embarrassed to admit such a thing. As though there is not more to life than a woman's virginity and its destruction, she often thinks to herself. She only allows herself to contemplate her lack of experience for a moment, however, lest it bring her down.

Any strong drink or recreational drug use?

No, Tasneem says. Pure as the driven snow.

The nurse ignores this comment. Your father, he was...

Tasneem waits for the nurse to finish, but the question just dangles there, incomplete, so she attempts to fill it in. A consult to the embassy, she offers.

The nurse looks perplexed. I'm sorry. I meant, your father's ethnicity was... what?

Oh, Tasneem says. Of course. My father was Asian.

His birthplace?

Seoul.

What year?

2009.

Before the detonation, then, the nurse says.

Tasneem is dumbfounded. The detonation was in 2042, she says. My father was not twenty-six when he died.

Right, of course, the nurse says. Although, I am -- sorry, I am perplexed about one thing.

Tasneem waits.

You said your father died in -- the nurse looks down at her documents -- 2068.

That's correct. Tasneem has an idea of where the nurse is going with this, but she remains quiet.

And you were born in -- the nurse consults the papers again -- 2075.

Yes, Tasneem says.

The nurse looks up. She doesn't say anything, just stares quizzically at Tasneem.

Tasneem waits.

Finally, the nurse says, I -- how -- I'm just confused.

My father preserved the necessary ingredients for life, Tasneem says. So that my mother could have a child, even if he was not present.

Ah, okay, the nurse says. You're an only child?

The first few tries didn't take, Tasneem says. I was conceived from the last batch. So yes, I'm an only child. My mother is fiercely loyal, and did not remarry.

The nurse smiles uncomfortably. Let's talk about your

mother, then. What year was she born?

2017, in Mumbai.

She was Indian, then?

Very much so.

Is she still alive?

No, ma'am. My mother died in 2087.

You were --

Twelve.

That's terrible, the nurse says.

Yes, ma'am.

Your mother was part of the first wave.

We both were, yes.

So she died on Ganymede, the nurse concludes. Not here on Aries.

Yes. Aries wasn't around until last year.

Right, the nurse says. I'm sorry. That's ridiculous of me.

It's okay, Tasneem says.

The nurse taps her pen on the paperwork. May I ask what from?

What from?

What did your mother die of? I'm sorry to be indelicate.

Tasneem says, My mother died because she was a creature of the Earth, and my father was buried there.

The nurse blinks. I -- I understand. It's just -- I need a cause of death for the, um, papers.

She died of respiratory failure, Tasneem answers.

The nurse notes this on the papers, then stands up. Tasneem stands as well, but the nurse says, No, please, sit. It may be a few minutes, but the doctor will want to interview you himself.

Is that standard? Tasneem asks.

You didn't think that the treatment was a simple pill you could take, did you? The nurse gathers the paperwork. No, every treatment requires a thorough investigation of your medical, emotional and psychological history, Ms. Kyoh. There's a bit more remaining, I'm afraid.

Tasneem sits down again. I wasn't told much, she says.

Generally it's a seven-week process, and then we administer the treatment or deny treatment permanently, the nurse says. You're at day one. I hope you're a patient woman.

Deny? Tasneem asks. Permanently?

The nurse nods. The doctor will tell you more. Can I bring you anything? Water?

No, thank you, Tasneem says.

Very well, the nurse says. Hold tight. He'll be here shortly.

Seven weeks? Ridiculous.

Tasneem stirs honey into her tea. I suppose it makes sense.

Sense how? Audra asks. I say if you're healthy and wealthy, you should get the treatment that same day. They're providing a service. You're the customer.

The customer hasn't always been right in fifty years, Tasneem says with a smile. Besides, I really do get it. Would you want to be responsible for making someone immortal who should not be?

Audra frowns. Like David? Because I'll tell you, that man

has no business making it to the end of the week, much less the end of the millennium.

No, not like David, Tasneem says. What if you were the doctor who immortalized a pathological killer, for example? What if Jack the Ripper ripped his way through six centuries of hapless young women because you didn't do your homework?

You know, it's really hard to win an argument when you make so much sense, Audra complains.

Tasneem walks to the kitchen and picks through her produce basket until she finds a grapefruit. She slices it in half, then holds one half up inquisitively.

Sure, Audra says.

Tasneem plucks two grapefruit spoons from the rack and returns to the table. How are you and David this week?

Audra chuckles bitterly. Do you think most people have to be asked that? How are you *this week*. Do you think most people get along for longer periods of time?

Maybe, Tasneem says. I think of you and David as a special case, though.

Special! Audra says. Why, because David's high-functioning, and I'm just this shrill, incompetent thing who happens to share his bed?

Because you're both lovely people, and you've fashioned a partnership that's lasted about a hundred years despite some pretty fundamental differences, Tasneem says.

Well, this week, David's a complete jerk, Audra says. And stop being so nice about him. You're supporting me right now.

Tasneem pokes her grapefruit. That's pretty disingenuous, Audra.

Oh, whatever, Audra says. Look, everybody wants to wallow and be selfish sometimes.

And this is your time?

This is my time, Audra agrees. If you don't want to support me unequivocally, that's fine. Your prerogative. You're smarter than me, after all. I'm sure you see right through this bullshit.

I am smarter than you, Tasneem allows with a smile.

Oh, it's like that, now, Audra says.

Not really.

Okay. Good.

It's all going to be fine, you know.

Audra sighs. I know. But it's nice to pretend sometimes that it isn't. It makes these mood swings feel a bit more logical.

Twenty-two weeks pregnant deserves a bit of a break in the logic department, I'd say.

Thanks, Neem. Audra sighs. You know, David's talking about taking the treatment, too.

David would make a great immortal, Tasneem says.

We're disagreed about it, though. Immortality is a little scary to me. Audra sips her tea. I mean, in a boring way. I don't know if I could find enough to keep me busy and happy for a few thousand years.

Sure, Tasneem says. I understand that. I worry a little about that, too.

Why? You're perfect for it. You'd get to see everything happen that you've been thinking about for the last twenty years.

Oh, yes, and that's why I'm trying for it, Tasneem says. But I'm not all about my work, you know. And I've never really known what to do with my free time. Studying people for so long has changed me. I can't watch a program without wondering what future versions of us might think of it. What would they learn about me by watching it?

You really can drain the joy out of anything, you know.

It's a talent, Tasneem says.

The doctor's working quarters are sparsely decorated. The seamed wall panels are stark and unwelcoming. He is one of the fortunate few with a window on the outer ring of Station Aries, and Tasneem's view at this very moment makes up for her bleak surroundings.

Aries turns like a great wheel over Earth. From Dr. Widla's office, Tasneem is overjoyed to see her mother's birthplace. India descends into the ocean like a great fang, although it is narrower than it once was, and flanked by several small islands that were once part of the mainland. Clouds stretch thin like shoestrings over the land, and are blown into taffeta as they cross the sea.

Humbling, yes?

Tasneem turns from the window as Dr. Widla enters the room. He's a stout man, perhaps in his late fifties, with a scruff of silvery beard hiding his mouth. Still, she recognizes a smile in his eyes, and returns it.

It's beautiful, she says. But only for a moment, and then it's horrifying.

I know just what you mean, Dr. Widla says. From time to

time we pass over my home, and I'm troubled to discover that it is somewhere beneath the ocean now. But it is oceanfront property now, is it not?

Tasneem laughs politely.

It's okay, you don't have to laugh. It is the most terrible joke I could say. Dr. Widla settles into the chair behind his desk, and indicates the chair near Tasneem. Please. Sit.

Tasneem reluctantly steps away from the window. Already India has moved on. She takes her seat and rests her hands nicely on her knees.

So, Dr. Widla says, turning slowly in his chair. You would like to live forever.

Well, not forever, Tasneem says. I know that's not really the case.

Ah, but you must not imagine only the now, Ms. Kyoh. You must consider the future, when you have lived for a century and someone has discovered a way to improve this treatment. What then? Will you take it? How will you feel about becoming truly immortal?

I suppose I won't know until I've been almost immortal, Tasneem says.

Dr. Widla studies her closely. Then he clasps his hands sharply. Tasneem flinches.

That's not a bad answer, he says, and his beard smiles at her again.

Shaken, Tasneem digs deep for a half-smile. Thank you.

So I'll begin here, Dr. Widla says. There are many things that the average person doesn't think about when they consider taking the treatment. For example, do they love their career? Will they be content to forestall retirement for several hundred years? That's a long time to work if you aren't in love with your work. Let's begin there. What will you do for income?

I've thought about this at length, Tasneem says. And I suppose the obvious answer would be that I could change careers at will, the treatment would provide me with ample time to discover new abilities or train for new experiences. There would be almost no limit on the number of careers I could experiment with.

Dr. Widla nods thoughtfully. But?

But I do genuinely love what I do, Tasneem confesses. I'm rather simple that way.

And what do you do?

Anthropology, she replies. I study us.

And what made you choose anthropology? From the great wheel of life and all of its choices, why that one? Why didn't you choose, say, baseball? Or terraforming? Or server at a restaurant?

Tasneem has been asked this question before. I've always been interested in what drives our behavior, she says. What led us to believe in gods for so long? Was it fear, or an overabundance of love? Why did we build roads? What was the purpose of the structures we created? I love stories, and there are countless stories in our history, and happening right now.

I see, Dr. Widla says. He picks up the documents prepared by the nurse the previous week, and makes a show of turning quickly through them. Then he drops them on the table again. I had theorized that it was because of your father.

Tasneem cocks her head to the side. My father?

Sure, Dr. Widla says. Why do any children grow up to choose what they do? With few exceptions, their reasons come from their parents. Why do you think I'm a doctor?

Why do you say my father? I don't see the connection.

Dr. Widla leans across the desk and clasps his hands together. You did not know him, yes?

Tasneem nods, her mouth suddenly dry. He died before I was born.

Quite some time before you were born, yes?

She nods again.

In a way, your father not only didn't live to see your birth and your great accomplishments as you became a woman -- but he didn't even know what he was going to miss out on. Forgive me if this seems direct, but your father died without a single thought of you in his head.

Tasneem's eyes have filled. That's not true, she says, voice trembling. My father planned for me.

Oh, yes, sure, Dr. Widla says, leaning back again. I did not mean to suggest that he didn't. But surely you can agree that your father planned for the *idea* of you, rather than you, specifically.

Tasneem turns her face.

My dear, I'm sorry, Dr. Widla says. Please don't cry. What I suggest is not that your father didn't care -- only that your father, sadly, did not have the opportunity to meet you, and didn't know what he was missing. If there is a clearer reason for that man's child to become a chronicler of human accomplishment, an investigator of human stories, I don't know what it might be.

The doctor moves to the chair beside Tasneem's. He hands

her a tissue.

Here, he says.

Tasneem takes it and dabs at her eyes. I'm sorry, she says.

No need, my dear, he says. It was not my intention to probe.

Tasneem nods, fighting the urge to cry again.

Do you know what your name means? Dr. Widla asks. I do. I looked it up. I always found Indian names to have such beautiful etymologies.

Tasneem says, It means *river*.

Dr. Widla says, Yes, but there's more. It means *river in heaven*.

I've never heard that before.

Rivers are like thread, he says. They stitch places together. They are seams that connect very different lands. I think it is lovely that you are an anthropologist. What better name for a woman who might herself be a river through time? he asks. You will have stability in your career once you are almost-but-not-quite godlike.

You're a philosopher as well as a doctor, Tasneem says.

Dr. Widla smiles. Time is always changing, and you will ride upon it, witnessing all of the great events that so many people will miss. So, Tasneem, you will probably not feel trapped as easily as a financier or a warehouse manager. Can you imagine spending four hundred years organizing inventory on a space dock?

Tasneem laughs.

You are bright, and I am charmed by you, Dr. Widla says. And so we shall do this.

Tasneem looks up at him, startled. But the nurse said it takes nearly two months to --

Pffft, Dr. Widla says, flapping a hand in the air. Sometimes you just know. We'll take care of the paperwork, and have you return in seven or eight weeks for the administering of the treatment. We can handle all of the extra steps on paper without running you through the grinder, he says, but unfortunately I cannot make time go any faster. That is the earliest we can manage.

Tasneem throws her arms around the doctor's neck. That's wonderful! she sobs.

You are still crying, he observes.

I'm sorry, she laughs, very nearly bawling.

Perhaps you will need all of my tissues, he says.

As Tasneem stands to leave, he says, Oh, please. One final thing.

What's that? she asks.

Be remarkably careful and thoughtful during these next few weeks, he says. Sometimes people who are approved seem to forget that they haven't had the treatment yet, and behave as if they are already nearly immortal.

Oh, no, Tasneem says. What happens to them?

Usually? They're run over by transports, or they forget to take spare oxygen cells when they work outside, he says. Dumb things. I can test for a lot of things, but sometimes pure dumb dumbness gets right by me. So you stay safe, and look both ways. Best if you simply strap yourself into your bunk until February.

Tasneem leaves the office with the doctor's words echoing in her head. Suddenly every step she takes is a possible broken ankle. Every corner she turns is an opportunity to be flattened by an oncoming pod. Every window is a potential airlock ready to fire her into space.

Her wrist vibrates, and she looks down to see a warm glow in the soft skin between her ulna and radius. She presses her thumb to the warm spot, and in her ear, a voice recording begins to play.

Neem! Come find me as soon as you're back, Neem. David -- well, David's gotten the treatment. I think something's wrong, but maybe you'd know better. Please hurry.

Tasneem wrinkles her nose. How could David have gotten the treatment?

Unless he bypassed the stability checks, like she had.

Except he would still have to wait seven weeks.

Black market, she thinks. *Oh, shit.*

She follows the concourse, passing the shops and common areas quickly. She had thought about celebrating her treatment approval by stopping for a pastry and spending some time in the green belt, but there's no time now. She bypasses the green belt as well, leaving its acres of gardens and streams and its lovely glass rooftop behind.

At the first juncture she comes to, Tasneem darts onto the inner ring and grabs a tether. The ring's momentum is startling, and she loses her balance, bumping roughly into a young man.

Sorry, she says.

He nods, and returns to his screenview.

Station Aries was built for efficiency. The lessons learned from Ganymede and Cassiopeia were both social and functional. Cassiopeia did away with the failed class-leveling experiment of Ganymede, but stumbled in its own way. The station was a vast labyrinth, a warren of cubbies and corridors and wings and sub-levels. Traveling anywhere could take hours, and there were stories of people becoming so hopelessly lost that they never found their way back to their quarters.

Aries solved that with a classic ring design. Residents called it the donut, or the wheel. It was not much different from the visionary concepts that scientists devised in the mid-twentieth century. Its interior was an effective series of rings that revolved at different speeds, and sometimes in different directions. The primary concourse was home to Aries's commercial interests, from shops to religious structures. Rotating at a slower speed one level below the concourse was a deep residential track, carefully planned to offer a variety of homes to the station's twenty-three million residents.

At junctures throughout the station, one could switch to a fast-track -- a ring that moved significantly faster than the other tracks, allowing for rapid transit between around the station. The ring never stopped, which made boarding and disembarking quite interesting. A grav-free track surrounded the ring, so that when someone stepped off of the fast-track, they would simply float. Of course, the fast-track's momentum was transferred to each passenger as they disembarked, and it was quite amusing to watch passengers flung into a zero-gravity space. The walls were deeply-cushioned to protect riders as they hurtled from the fast-track.

Boarding was never easy, though. One simply had to go for it, and hope for the best.

Tasneem holds to the tether, and with her free hand, taps her wrist. Audra, she says.

Her implant responds almost immediately. Audra is unavailable, it says.

David, she says.

David is unavailable.

Shit, Tasneem says.

The young man with the screenview glances up at her briefly, then away.

Locate Audra, Tasneem says.

Audra is unavailable.

Locate David, goddammit, she says.

David is --

Unavailable. Alright. Shit. She thinks for a moment. Dr. Widla, she says.

One moment, her implant responds.

Come on, come on, Tasneem urges.

Dr. Widla's office, a female voice answers.

Dr. Widla, please. It's Tasneem Kyoh, and it's an emergency.

Okay, calm down, please, the woman says. Can you tell me --

I don't have time. Please, Tasneem says. Tell him that a friend has had the treatment, and I believe it may be a black market strain. I'm going to him now and I need Dr. Widla's help.

The doctor does not treat patients who have acquired the treatment in out-of-office experiments, the woman's voice says. I'm sorry, but --

Please. Listen to me. The man who took the treatment is David Dewbury.

I'm sorry, did you say --

Yes. I did. And you'll understand now why this is important, so please, please, tell Dr. Widla to call me. It's very urgent. We cannot let anything happen to him. Am I clear?

The David D--

Yes. Yes! Tell him! Tasneem cries, and presses her wrist to disconnect.

The young man behind her taps her shoulder.

What? she says, rattled.

Did you say David Dewbury had a black market treatment? Do you know how dangerous that is?

If you eavesdropped on that much, then you must have heard the rest of my conversation, Tasneem says. So yes, I fucking know.

Wow, the young man says. Excuse me. I was just going to say, I might be able to help.

Tasneem's anger vanishes. How? How?

I think I know where he might be.

I don't have time to be lied to, Tasneem warns.

I'm not lying. I'm Blair Hudgens.

Tasneem's expression is blank.

Blair Hudgens, the young man repeats. Oh, never mind. I'm a pulse journalist. I did a piece about illegal treatment scams last week. So I'm not lying. You can trust me. I really do think

I can take you to him.

Tasneem nods. Please. Now, please.

Okay. We'll get off at juncture seven.

Juncture seven? Tasneem says. That's --

The Upper Ward. I know. Please trust me.

Okay, Tasneem says. I sure do hope you're real.

Oh, I'm real, Blair mutters. I just hope I'm right. I'm Blair, by the way.

You said that already.

I know, I was just hoping you'd forget and tell me your name.

Maybe later, Tasneem says.

Blair raises his eyebrows.

Fine, she says. Tasneem. I'm Tasneem. Can we get moving?

The Upper Ward is a direct response to the class-leveling failure of Station Ganymede and the clutter of Station Cassiopeia. On Earth, the Upper Ward might have been a gated neighborhood of multi-million-dollar estates. On Station Aries, the Upper Ward is a sleeve that cups the outer ring of the station. It follows the rotation of Aries itself, though at a slower speed.

Access to the Ward is limited to station officials and residents, which would explain how David gained entry. Audra was one of the first administrators brought to Aries.

Most of the black markets are run from here, Blair says.

Tasneem follows as closely as she can. She's distracted by the opaque glass buildings and what looks like real grass carefully blanketed at their feet. The canopy over the Ward is electronically tinted, filtering the view through a color that corresponds with the time of day back on Earth. Right now the canopy is a brilliant gold touched with blue.

There are even artificial clouds bobbing across the artificial sky.

The stench of entitlement here is overpowering. At this moment, Tasneem sort of wants to punch out the first Ward resident she sees.

You said something, she says.

I said that most of the markets are run from here, Blair repeats.

How is that -- but -- why?

Blair is hard to keep pace with. Where's the last place you would look for a black marketeer?

Here, I guess, Tasneem says.

That's partly true, Blair answers. When you look for the guy dealing the shit, yeah, you're right. He's not here. But when you start connecting the shit to the money? It almost always leads to places like this.

He glances back at her as they run through the Ward, which almost feels abandoned. She hasn't seen a single person here since they entered.

You still look uncertain, Blair says.

I just --

You just thought that the Ward was more noble than that, he finishes.

She nods.

Don't worry about it, he says. Everybody thinks that.

Where is everybody?

He looks around. You're right. Kind of quiet today, isn't it.

Not kind of. It's completely silent.

Well, they're the upper-upper-upper class, he says. They have people to go outside for them, so why should they? Their views are better than anything on the rest of Aries.

Yeah, but -- don't they work? Or socialize?

Maybe not, Blair says. Nobody had to give up their wealth or status when they came to Aries. It's not like Ganymede was. You know?

Tasneem says, Yeah, I do.

Blair points. That's where we're going.

If he's anywhere, it's most likely there, Blair says.

He's steering them towards a narrow glass structure, several stories high. While the other residences are marked with identity plates, this one has no such marking. There's a personal deck parked in front of it, but nobody is inside.

What is this place? Tasneem asks. Have you been here?

I've never been inside, Blair says. But this is where William Bogleman lives.

Tasneem stops dead. Bogleman.

Uh huh, Blair says.

As in Harvey Bogleman.

Uh huh.

This is his son's house? His son lives on Aries?

Uh huh.

Tasneem paces on the lawn. I really don't believe it. I thought that Harvey was the only Bogleman off-world.

He was, Blair says. But he's not anymore. Now William is the only Bogleman off-world.

And you think David's inside?

Blair nods. I'm quite sure of it, actually. William would have wanted to do this one himself. It's David Dewbury, after all.

Himself? Are you saying he administers the treatment himself? Tasneem is dumbfounded. Is he a doctor?

He's a socialite, Blair says. He throws parties. You know, like socialite boys do.

Okay, tell me and tell me now, Tasneem says, stepping close to Blair. How dangerous are the black market treatments?

They're bad, Tasneem. Scale of one to ten? These are a twenty. That report I did -- we looked for survivors to interview, and we found three. Two wouldn't talk, and the third one -- well, the third one had some sort of relapse, and figured she had nothing to lose. So she talked. And then she died.

Jesus, Tasneem says. We have to go in.

Blair hangs back. I'm not sure.

Did you bring me all the way here just to stop? My friend is inside, and he might be dying! And did I mention he's the most brilliant man alive right now? Or at least probably? We are not, not, not letting him go. Now take me inside.

Blair nods. Alright. But --

No, no. No buts, nothing. Inside. You have to help me.

Blair leads Tasneem to the residence entry. I've never been

inside, he says again.

It's a rich person's house, Tasneem says. How dangerous can it be?

That's what worries me, Blair says. Look.

She follows his gaze to the doorstep. There's an insignia there, etched into the hard surface.

H, she says. Okay.

You don't recognize that? he asks.

Should I? What's it stand for?

Blair looks genuinely nervous. It stands for Harvard, he says.

As in Harvard Club? Tasneem asks.

He nods.

Shit, she says.

FIRST WAVE

Tasneem held her mother's hand tightly. The spaceport's processing facility was a bustling hive of activity, and smelled sour. All around her were strangers, most in dirty clothing, with mud caked on their skin. More than a few were injured, and some appeared to be barely holding themselves upright. They stank, and their eyes were tired and sunken. Most wore the same blank expression, the stunned look of people from whom almost everything had been taken. They were widows and widowers, orphans and strays, cast-offs and forgotten.

Tasneem, tuck tuck! her mother said when Tasneem lagged behind.

A harsh female voice droned over a makeshift public address system: IF YOU HAVE BELONGINGS, DEPOSIT THEM IN THE STACKS UNDER THE BLUE SIGN. NO PERSONAL BELONGINGS ARE PERMITTED THROUGH THESE GATES.

Tasneem stood on her tiptoes and leaned this way and that, trying to see what was under the blue sign. In tiny flickers between stragglers she saw it: a heaping pile of satchels and suitcases and backpacks and push-carts and wheelchairs and buckets and toys.

Amma, Tasneem said.

Her mother kept pulling her forward in the crowd.

Amma, she repeated. Amma!

Her mother looked over her shoulder. Tasneem, come! Hurry.

Amma, why are all the bags left?

But her mother kept tugging her along.

RESTRICTIONS FOR ENTRY ARE AS FOLLOWS, the woman's voice blared. CHILDREN UNDER THE AGE OF FOUR ARE NOT PERMITTED. ADULTS OVER THE AGE OF FIFTY-FIVE ARE ALSO NOT PERMITTED. ALL APPLICANTS MUST PROVIDE PROOF OF IDENTITY. IF YOU DO NOT HAVE YOUR PASSCARD OR YOUR IMPRINT I.D., PLEASE STEP OUT OF LINE NOW.

Someone behind Tasneem screamed.

She looked back up at her mother.

Amma, she said.

But her mother only pulled her deeper into the crowd.

What will happen to them, Amma?

Tasneem rested her chin on the window sill and stared down at the throngs of muddy people below.

They have been turned away, darling, her mother said.

But why? There are still empty seats.

It's true, her mother agreed. But I think they have their reasons. Maybe there isn't enough room on the space station. Maybe just this transport vessel is large, but our destination is small.

Why weren't we turned away? Tasneem asked.

Her mother shook her head. Be grateful that we were not, she said. The people below us, they do not have homes to return to. They will probably never go to space. They will have hard lives.

It's not fair, Tasneem said.

No, her mother agreed. It isn't fair. But much in life is not fair, Tasneem. You will be reminded of this from time to time. Better to accept it now, when you are young, than to discover it when you are an old woman like me.

You aren't old, Amma! Tasneem threw her arms around her mother.

Oh, Tasneem, her mother said. I am. You don't know it, but there was a time when a woman had to be careful having babies at my age. I was much older than most mothers.

How old were you?

Fifty-eight, her mother replied. But when I was born -- a long, long time ago -- it was considered risky for a woman older than forty to have a child. Thank your stars for science, Tasneem. It found a way to bring you to me.

Would Baap have liked me, Amma?

Her mother smiled and touched Tasneem's cheek. Your father would have cherished you. He would have loved this, too. To go to space! With you and with me! We will have to think of him always, Tasneem. We cannot forget him.

Show me his picture again.

Her mother looked around, and then produced a tiny paper photograph from beneath her robe. The paper was wrinkled and folded, and its color was beginning to fade from the creases.

Don't let anyone see, she cautioned.

I won't, Tasneem said.

Tasneem studied the photograph for the hundredth time. Her father was young when it was taken, with expressive eyes tucked beneath kind eyebrows. His hair was windswept, as if he had just stepped off of a sailboat.

He looks like me, she said.

Her mother nodded.

Tasneem turned the photograph over. The writing was worn, but still readable.

For Anjali, my love.
-Jae

Tasneem kissed the photo, and then pressed it against the window.

So you can see it one last time, she said.

She held the photo for a long moment, then handed it back to her mother, whose eyes sparkled.

Okay, Tasneem said. We can go now.

In the late afternoon, the spaceport in northern Washington seemed to inhale sharply.

All activity paused. The commotion within the crowd of refused applicants died down. Spaceport officials and staff halted what they were doing. Reporters stood quietly as cameras rolled. There were no loudspeaker countdowns, no showmanship. This was not a grand day of human achievement. This was a day of desperate actions.

The first blast of heat rolled thick and heavy across the launch platform, then surged across the wide empty facility before it broke like an angry summer day. The crowd of applicants blinked and stepped backward, and when they returned to their homes later, the mud on their skin had been cooked away, and their skin had been browned. Still they remained, sweating in the lingering shimmery blur that engulfed them.

Through that haze they watched mournfully as their lifeboat lifted into the sky.

It seemed to move in slow motion, shedding the Earth like an unnecessary skin. It was a hulking, unattractive beast, this lifeboat, its bulk standing on thin rocket spindles that glowed white as they pushed the Earth away.

It rose into the sky like an appliance, shaky and obese, covered with blinking lights of red and blue and gold.

And then the secondary rockets flared with a resounding *crack*, and the ship ripped through the clouds and was gone.

The heat remained for a time.

The crowd, permanently Earthbound, were slower to leave. Nobody seemed ready to admit it was over, and they had failed to make it. It was as if god himself had returned to

Earth, and had carried away just a handful of people. The rest milled about, purposeless. Most had nowhere to go. Some would kill themselves that very day, joined by other strangers rejected by spaceports all around the planet.

What reason to live could be left?

Earth's remnants slowly began to drown.

Tasneem and Anjali sat together, snuggled close.

Nobody in the passenger space had spoken. They gathered together around the windows and stared quietly down at the Earth as it fell away beneath them. The booster rockets disengaged and pinwheeled towards the seas below. It seemed as though the passengers were holding their breath.

When the blue sky dimmed, and then turned black, the atmosphere within the ship changed, too.

There were six thousand of them aboard. They were each freshly washed, and dressed in white linen robes. They were not unlike angels summoned into the heavens. All that was left was the unwrapping of their wings.

Tasneem looked up at her mother's pretty face.

Amma, she said. We made it?

Almost, her mother said.

Almost, Tasneem repeated. But soon?

Very soon, her mother said.

How do you say it again?

Gah-neh-mead.

Ganymede.

Very good.

It's pretty.

Her mother nodded. Let's close our eyes and rest now, she said.

While Anjali slept, Tasneem remained awake and stared through the window. She could not see any stars, but she could see part of the Earth, a swirled marble hanging in a sea of blackness.

And at a great distance, she could see tiny sparks following her into the sky.

Ships, she thought. Ships like mine.

On that day, one hundred ships had set out for Ganymede. In the next six weeks, those ships would return to the Earth, scoop up more passengers, and return to the space station.

Tasneem closed her eyes.

The first wave of settlers were away.

DAVID

And then what happened?

My doctor contacted me -- I had called him earlier. I didn't really know who to talk to -- I was panicked, I guess.

Did he come to the Upper Ward to meet you?

He did.

But he was too late.

We were all too late.

When you arrived, David Dewbury was already dead.

Yes.

Did your doctor -- Doctor Emil Widla, is that correct?

That's -- yes. Doctor Widla.

Did he say how Mr. Dewbury had died?

Objection. Secondhand.

I'll rephrase. Doctor Widla expressed an opinion about Mr. Dewbury's cause of death, is that correct?

Yes.

And what did Dr. Widla say?

He said -- he said that David had been given Amrita.

Amrita. Not Soma?

No. Not Soma.

Did you ask him what Amrita was?

I did.

And what did he say?

He said that Amrita was a biologically-corrupt strain of Soma.

Did you ask what that meant?

He told me. I don't think I asked.

What did he say about it?

He said that Soma enhanced your DNA, but that Amrita was like white noise. He said it scrambled your DNA.

Scrambled your DNA.

Yes. That's what he said.

Ms. Kyoh, did you see Mr. Dewbury inside the residence?

Yes.

And what was his condition?

Please don't make me say.

Ms. Kyoh, please answer the question.

I -- he -- goddammit. He looked like something inside of him had exploded. It was horrible.

Like some sort of bomb?

No. Not like a bomb, not like with shrapnel or anything. It was like -- it was like a dye pack had exploded inside of him.

How do you mean?

Just under his skin, all over his body, everything had turned an awful purple-black. Like he had rotted inside, and you could almost see through his skin.

And how long did Dr. Widla think he had been dead?

Objection. Speculative.

Overruled. Continue.

Let me ask again. How long did Dr. Emil Widla think that Mr.

Dewbury had been dead?

He said David had been dead for probably fifteen minutes.

Fifteen minutes. And his condition, did that look recent to you?

Jesus. He looked like -- it was like he had been dead for days. It was so awful.

And can you tell us, while you were in the residence, did you see any sign of Mr. Bogleman?

No. It was like nobody lived there at all. It was completely empty.

And the glass walls, were they transparent when you entered?

No. They were opaque.

So it was dark inside.

Mostly, yes.

And you're sure you didn't see Mr. Bogleman?

I'm positive. It was just David.

What about Mrs. Dewbury? She wasn't present?

No. Audra wasn't there.

But you saw her later?

They haven't allowed me to see her.

By they, you mean the hospital staff, correct?

Yes. Nobody will let me see her. She must be so scared.

And why is Mrs. Dewbury in the hospital?

I don't know.

You were told something, though.

Yes.

What was it?

I was told that she had suffered a mental break.

Administrator Dewbury.

Yes.

And do you believe that to be true?

I don't know. I can't see her. She's a strong woman, but --

But?

If that had happened to my significant other, I probably would have had a mental break as well.

Ms. Kyoh, one last question. Do you still intend to have the treatment? Do you still intend to take Soma?

I --

Please answer the question.

I do. Yes, I do.

No more questions. Thank you, Ms. Kyoh.

The deposition is broadcast throughout the fleet -- not only on Aries, but on Ganymede and Cassiopeia, too. Within minutes of its ending, Tasneem's wrist is vibrating ceaselessly. She presses until the vibrations stop, and exhales slowly. She's standing in a surprisingly quiet room on the eighth level of the attorney's office, looking down at the concourse below. There's a small crowd, most of them journalists. There are a few blogbots hovering at the edge of the gathering.

She'll wait a few minutes to see how many leave.

The lawyer who interviewed her leans into the room. Tasneem, are you okay?

Tasneem turns. Just taking a moment before I go outside. There's not a back entrance or anything, is there?

I'm sorry, no. I'm afraid I'll need this room in about ten minutes, unfortunately.

Tasneem says, Of course.

The lawyer nods and ducks out of the room again.

On the concourse she can see a few signs, but she's too high to read them. There aren't enough people gathered to make a scene, but she's dreading the gauntlet anyway. She's never been a person of interest to the media before, and she's reluctant to begin now.

She bows her head. If only Audra was here with her now.

And poor, sad David.

She doesn't allow herself to cry.

Not in this room. Not until she is home, in her quiet apartment with its quiet walls and its cool floors and pale light. There, in her safest place, she will mourn her friend.

Blair is in the lobby, but she almost walks right by him.

Tasneem, he says, touching her hand.

She stops. Oh. Hey.

Hey. You okay? That was -- that seemed difficult.

You saw it?

I think everybody saw it. David was pretty important to these people.

Tasneem looks past Blair to the crowd outside. Yeah, she says.

You alright? he asks again.

She shifts her focus to Blair. Are you asking as a friend or as a journalist?

Well, not as a journalist. Are we friends?

They don't look like they're going to be very nice to me, she says, nodding towards the reporters waiting outside.

Maybe not, Blair agrees. They don't know you like I do.

You don't know me at all, Tasneem says.

Well, *yet*.

I don't know what that means, Tasneem says. You're bothering me.

I can help get you through the crowd, if you like.

She eyes Blair suspiciously. How?

There, Blair announces. Pretty good, huh?

That snarky bitch, Tasneem says. She lied to me.

Blair turns around in the doorway. What?

Nothing. The lawyer, Tasneem says. She said there wasn't another exit.

And you believed her? You ever hear of something called a fire code? Been around for a few million years, still governs how buildings have to handle escape routes?

Shut up, says Tasneem, but she smiles.

Alright, Blair says. A smile. Nice.

He steps back and holds the door for her. Tasneem pokes her head out. They've emerged in a quiet corridor between the law firm and the tower beside it. There are no reporters in sight.

That was pretty cool, Tasneem says.

Miss Kohhhh!

Look out! Blair says, snatching Tasneem back from the doorway. A blogbot dives in too fast and almost collides with the door. The bot wings it, and ricochets out into the concourse, where it's clipped by a boy on a personal deck.

The bot hits the ground with a metallic thunk, bounces a few times, and stops. The screen on its face points toward the sky.

Miss Kohhhh, it squeals again. *A few words! Where are you? What happened?*

Tasneem steps forward without thinking.

Wait a second there, Blair says, taking her arm. What are you doing?

Tasneem shakes her head to clear the cobwebs. Instinct, I guess.

It's not a real person, Blair says. I mean -- well, yes, okay, it is. But that's just a floating avatar for some blogger back in his apartment.

How do you know it's a he? Tasneem says.

Well, Blair says. I guess because it sounded like a guy's voice? Also, I saw the screen before it hit the door. Skinny kid, red hair. Blogger.

I hate journalists, Tasneem says, picking up her bag from the ground.

Hold up there, Blair says. You're talking to one.

I was specifically talking about that one, Tasneem says, pointing at the sputtering bot. And those vultures who were waiting to pounce on me.

Okay, two things now, Blair says. One, I'm a journalist. That thing -- he points at the bot -- is most definitely not. And two, you don't know anything about wildlife. Vultures? That pounce? Where did you study, on Neptune?

They don't have vultures on Neptune, Tasneem says. Can we go now, please?

Alright, fine, Blair says. But if there are vultures on Neptune, I'm pretty sure they don't pounce there, either.

Shut up, Tasneem says.

Bound, maybe, but pounce? Not likely.

From the concourse, Blair and Tasneem catch the fast-track to juncture three. Blair makes a move to stand beside Tasneem, but she turns and says, I'd really like a few moments to myself.

Okay, Blair says.

It's just that -- okay, today's been a little rough. And I really appreciate you getting me past the reporters, but I just need some quiet time.

Okay, Blair says.

It's nothing personal.

I didn't think it was, Blair says.

Tasneem studies him for a moment. I'm going to go stand over there.

I'll be standing right here.

She smiles. Thank you.

The fast-track hums along. Tasneem leans on a window and exhales. From here she can see across the gap that forms the central hole in Aries's ring design. The far side of Aries is a thin ribbon, distant and small. As rapidly as the fast-track moves, it will take almost an hour to reach juncture three.

She closes her eyes.

She almost drifts into sleep, and then she remembers the calls that she had missed. Without opening her eyes, she presses her wrist, then squeezes twice to begin playback of the recordings logged. Unsurprisingly, there are more than twenty messages, and most of them are from reporters and strangers. One is even from Blair, telling her that he'd be waiting for her in the lobby of the attorney's building.

The reporters want the same thing -- exclusives.

Fat lot of good an exclusive will do you when I've just had my deposition broadcast to the entire fleet, Tasneem thinks.

The next few messages are just the same.

Miss Kyoh, a few questions.

Tasneem, our viewers are interested in you.

We'd like to get inside the relationship you had with David Dewbury and Audra Salter.

Please call.

Call us immediately.

Let's meet for coffee and discuss what this means for you.

She sighs.

The next message is from David.

Tasneem. It's David.

She listens to the message again and again, and the shock doesn't seem to wear off. It can't be real, can it? How could it possibly be real?

There's only one reason you're receiving this message. I'm sorry. I know you liked me. I liked you, too. I had a feeling the treatment might go badly, and I should have waited for a better option for myself, I know I should have -- but I couldn't.

You goddamn selfish bastard! Tasneem screams inside of her own head.

I know what you're thinking.

She cannot wait until she is in her apartment. His voice brings the tears out of her. She cries quietly, listening.

You're thinking I should have the treatment done like everybody else. For real. In a doctor's office. That's what you're thinking, isn't it?

Even though she's heard the message six times already, she still nods. Yes, that's what I'm thinking. Yes. Yes.

Tasneem, I wanted to. It wasn't the money -- it was expensive, but you know we would have found a way. It wasn't that. There was -- well, I had other reasons. They would never have given me the treatment. Not me. Not for real.

What reasons? she shouts.

And so I've made a bad call, and I must be gone now. This message is triggered by my death. You're maybe wondering now: why didn't he send this to Audra? Well, I can't explain that. I chose you. Maybe you know why.

But she didn't.

There's something important that you need to see, David continues. *If you're at home, then you're there already. Follow these instructions...*

GANYMEDE

They met, all three of them, when they were twelve years old. They had come up through different educational channels, each of them from a different arm of Ganymede. The space station was an enormous cross, like a massive tire iron circling Earth slowly, and each of its four arms was a complete city unto itself. Of the four arms, three are named for the Jovian moons which are sisters to Ganymede itself -- Io, Europa and Callisto. The fourth arm is named Galileo, for the astronomer who discovered the moons in 1610.

Tasneem had always found it disorderly to name a four-pronged space station for a single moon of a quartet, and then come up short when naming its components. It felt dramatically wrong that the station itself was not named for Galileo. That would have made more sense, she thought, and then the four cities could have been named Ganymede, Io, Europa and Callisto. That felt proper, and a nice tribute to a dead old man.

Instead, the dead old man took a back seat to one of the chunks of rock that he had discovered.

It just wasn't right.

Audra came from Io. She lived with her grandparents and an uncle. Her parents had been evangelicals who believed that Earth was sacred and the future home of their personal deity, and refused to emigrate to Ganymede. They'd had the opportunity, and had turned it down. Her grandfather often referred to Audra's parents -- his own daughter and son-in-law -- as damned fools. Tasneem liked him.

Tasneem, of course, lived with her mother in Callisto City. They shared a small compartment on the interior causeway, far from the picturesque outer residences. Of course, the station administration insisted that all residences were equal, that in fact all residents themselves were equal, but Tasneem knew that could never be true.

Audra had thought her pessimistic, but David had agreed with her. Equality, he would sometimes say, is a myth even in cultures that acknowledge and promote it.

David had always sounded smart. He *was* smart, but he talked smart. Tasneem didn't know anybody else like him. He was from Europa City, and while Tasneem and Audra played after classes released, David took the station line to Galileo City University, where he sat with the professors and talked for hours. They call me stunningly bright, he confided to Tasneem once. But I think it's just that they're surprisingly limited in their vision. I thought professors were supposed to be smarter than everybody else, but this has just taught me that no matter how high you climb, there will always be people who shouldn't be there with you.

David lived alone, and somehow managed to do so without attracting the attention of Ganymede Administration, which surely would have placed him with a guardian pair. He never talked to Audra or Tasneem about his parents, or whether they even came to Ganymede with him in the first place.

Audra and Tasneem each knew that David was going to be special. There was no question which of them he would end up with -- Audra was visibly interested, and clung to him in a way that Tasneem was incapable of. She seemed quite content to -- well, to *serve* him. Audra understood, Tasneem often thought, that David was on some plane above her, always thinking, always contemplating. Without her, David would forget the most basic human needs. So Audra cared for him, and David mostly didn't acknowledge Audra's ministrations.

Tasneem loved him. This was never a secret. Audra understood this, and wasn't bothered by it. To her, Tasneem was too similar to David. If the two of them were ever together, they would have one explosively intellectual year together -- then die of malnutrition and lack of exercise.

The social circle that they would dance in for the next twenty-one years was decided.

I'm not going, David said.

Oh, come on, Davy, come on, you have to go! Audra insisted. *Please*, please, please go. Please.

Tasneem laughed, trailing behind the two of them as they walked through the corridors of Ursa Academy. She and Audra had taken the station line to the school to meet David. They had waited outside David's classroom, Audra peeking in the windows repeatedly to try to get his attention. He's just so *serious*, she had complained. He won't look up at *all*.

Do you think I should go? David asked, looking over his shoulder at Tasneem. He pretended not to notice Audra, who had draped herself over his arm and was practically limp, her feet almost dragging along the corridor behind her.

Don't ask me, Tasneem said.

But I am asking you.

Audra popped up. Yeah, Tasneem. He should go, right? He should go.

I don't know, Tasneem said. Do you want to go?

Oh, man, no, Audra said, throwing her hands over her face. Don't ask him *that*.

No, David said.

See? Audra said.

Well, then you shouldn't go, Tasneem said.

Tasneem says I don't have to go, David said.

Yeah. I heard. Audra shot a withering look at Tasneem, who just shrugged.

They're supposed to be the best band in the whole world, Audra whined. Come *on-nnn*.

How do you know they're the best band in the world? David asked. What were the criteria? Did someone perform critical studies? What were the characteristics determined to be *best*? Is a consistent voice the best indicator of the best band? Or is experimentation a more appropriate --

David. God, Audra said. Come on, Tasneem. Let's go.

Audra dropped David's hand like a hot rock and stomped up the corridor.

Tasneem caught up to David and said, I'm sorry she's like that.

David smiled. It's okay, he said. As long as she is free to be like that, and I am free to be like this, we will always both be happy.

That doesn't sound like it works out well for her, Tasneem said. Works out pretty good for you, though.

It only doesn't work for her because she requires another person to achieve happiness, David said. She'll either grow out of that or she won't. If she does, she'll be happy.

Sometimes I don't think you're twelve years old, Tasneem said.

David smiled again. Sometimes, he whispered, I think I'm twelve thousand.

Tas*neem*, Audra complained.

Audra stomped her foot in indignation.

Gotta go, Tasneem said.

I really meant those questions, David said. See if you can determine why they're the best band in the world. It presents some interesting logical conflicts that must be winnowed through.

They're the best band because Audra wants you to go with her, Tasneem said. We probably won't even go now. She just wants to be with you.

But I'm going to University now, David said.

I know. She just wants to feel like she's more important than what you're doing.

But she isn't, David said.

Tasneem whispered, I wouldn't tell her that part.

She skipped ahead and joined Audra.

How can a band be the best band in the world if you live on a space colony, and not on a planet? David said to himself, walking along. Do they mean the word *world* literally? Or is it a loose term that can be applied to any social construct in which you reside? If that's the case, then our space colony is a world. By the same logic, a community of spacedivers who float together through the cosmos without anything but each other could also be a world.

The girls vanished ahead, and David continued to walk to the station line, talking to himself.

Audra had still wanted to go to the show, and so Tasneem had gone along. The band was certainly not the best band on any world, Tasneem thought, and she knew she would have a fun conversation with David later about what really would constitute the best band, and whether you could even truly identify such a thing.

David liked objective conversations about subjective things.

He's so difficult, Audra complained.

They were on the station line from the venue in Galileo City. The cylindrical transport moved slowly through the center of the Galilean arm, only slightly faster than the walking speed of the few people outside. The entire car was a crystal lit from the inside. Tasneem felt exposed on the station line, but she never noticed anybody outside watching her.

He never wants to do *anything*, Audra continued.

Tasneem had had enough. That's not true.

Oh, no? When is the last time he agreed to come to anything with me?

You said he never wants to do anything, Tasneem pointed out. But really, David always wants to do something. You just don't like the things he does. Maybe if you really wanted to spend time with him, you would join him for the things he's interested in.

Audra folded her arms. Yeah, but those things are really boring. And anyway, he should show me that I'm more important than that.

Whatever, Tasneem said.

Audra grabbed Tasneem's knees and leaned forward. Neemy, she said. He should. I'm really special. I know I am. And he should make me feel that way.

If you already know you are, then why is that his job? Tasneem asked.

Now it was Audra's turn. Whatever, she said.

Tasneem enjoyed a measure of silence.

Then Audra caved again, and turned back to her. Look, she insisted. David's just so smart.

So?

So I want to know that he's smart enough to know what he's got, Audra said.

I don't even know what that means, Tasneem replied. David doesn't *have* you. He doesn't own you.

I'm his girlfriend.

So?

Stop saying so! Audra exclaimed. Look, I'm his girlfriend,

and he should treat me more like -- like --

Like what? The Queen of Spain?

No, I can wait until I'm married to be his queen, Audra said. But right now I should be his princess.

Tasneem sighed. Audra. Listen to me. I'm going to explain something that you don't get, because if I don't, you'll never ever be with David forever. I know you want that, so you have to listen to me.

Audra exhaled in frustration. Look, I --

Audra. Listen to me. David is not like every other boy you've ever know. Don't you see that? David doesn't have a romantic bone in his body. And even if he did, he's twelve years old. He has plenty of time to be romantic later if he wants to. But he won't be, because David is like a robot. He just wants to consume knowledge. He wants to know everything. David wants to be the person in the world who knows everything about everything, because that's who David is. Do you understand? You will never be more important to him than a conversation he'll have with someone who knows something he doesn't know.

Audra began to cry.

Tasneem pinched her eyes shut and took a long, slow breath. Audra, look at it this way, she started.

No! No, I won't look at it your way, Audra said. Your way sucks, Tasneem. And just because you don't have a boyfriend, don't try to screw up what I have. And don't screw things up with me, either, because I know boys, I know lots of boys, and I can probably convince one of them to be your boyfriend or something.

Gee, thanks, Tasneem said. But you're completely missing

my point.

No, you're missing *mine*, Audra said. And it's too bad, because this is my stop, and now we're not friends.

Okay, Tasneem said.

Audra had been in the middle of rushing off of the train, anxious to have the final word. But Tasneem's acceptance had stopped her short.

You're just like him, Audra said in a wounded voice. It's like I don't really matter to either one of you.

The car's door began to close.

No, no, Audra said, and she squeezed through the narrowing space. Then she stood outside the car and watched as it hummed slowly away, carrying Tasneem with it.

Tasneem turned her attention back to the view ahead, and her long, slow ride to Callisto City. She wasn't worried about Audra. These tantrums usually passed, and they would be friends again in a few days. Instead, she thought about the band. They hadn't been good, although there had been a woman playing a slide guitar, and Tasneem had closed her eyes during the woman's solo and been transported to a quiet, mournful place. She liked it.

Tasneem's pocket vibrated.

Her eyes snapped open -- she hadn't realized that she had closed them -- and she retrieved her wristband from her jacket and put it on. She had forgotten that she'd removed it. She tapped the top of the band, and answered the incoming call.

Tasneem?

It was David.

He had been on the ground outside her compartment when she finally arrived. He had a tablet on his knees, and was furiously writing things.

David? she asked.

He kept writing, so she waited. A few minutes passed, and still she waited.

Finally he put the tablet down. Tasneem, he said. I'm sorry. It's late.

It's not too bad, she said. Come inside.

He got to his feet and followed her through the door.

Mom? Tasneem called. I'm home. David's here.

Anjali appeared in the doorway of the sleeping quarters. David, she said. Hello.

You should tell her what you told me, Tasneem said.

Anjali looked at her daughter, then back at David. Is something wrong?

David looked at the floor. Mrs. Kyoh, I have been living alone.

Anjali nodded. I know. Tasneem has told me. She says you are a very grown-up boy, and that she knows you are not in danger on your own. I believe her.

So far the Station Administration didn't know, Tasneem interjected.

David looked away.

David? Anjali asked, not unkindly. How did that escape

their notice?

Tasneem touched his shoulder. It's okay to tell her.

Anjali waited patiently. She looked very tired, which worried Tasneem a little. It was not that late, and her mother had looked more and more weary the past few months.

David looked at the floor. I found my way into their system, he confessed. And I invented records for my parents, and assigned them to my compartment.

Anjali nodded. And was that difficult?

David brightened. Not at all! In fact, the most difficult thing about it was trying to think of names for my fake parents.

Tasneem laughed.

Anjali smiled. David?

He went silent and looked at her.

Where are your parents, actually?

David bit his lip.

It's okay, Tasneem said.

Anjali nodded again.

David's shoulders slumped. I don't have parents. I'm an orphan.

And you found a way onto Ganymede despite this? Anjali asked.

Yes, David said.

You're a smart boy, David.

He smiled hesitantly. Thank you.

Tell me what has happened that has you so worried.

Tasneem nudged him.

I --

David faltered. He looked helplessly at Tasneem.

Tasneem looked at her mother. They've found him out, Amma.

Tasneem and David waited in the lobby. David chewed his nails, stopping only when Tasneem chided him, then starting again as soon as she looked away.

Tasneem looked at the sign behind the reception table.

Junior Citizen Services.

There was no more terrifying place for David, she knew.

Anjali was in the office across the room, meeting with JCS administrators as well as top Station Administration officials. There was no easy way to predict what might happen. No citizen had ever hacked his way into station databases to falsify citizenship. And since this had happened both on Earth and Ganymede, the authorities were struggling with jurisdiction.

Tasneem feared the worst -- that David would be shipped back to Earth.

You can't let that happen, Amma, she had told her mother before the meeting. Look at him. He's terrified. He wouldn't last a week down there. Please help him.

Tasneem placed her hands on David's. Stop chewing them, she said again.

He gave her a guilty look. I don't know if I can. They're going to send me --

Nobody's going to send you anyplace, Tasneem said. Amma

will solve it for you.

I don't mean anything by this, but your mother is just a citizen, David said. She can't actually fix this. They're going to deport me to Earth and I'm going to drown or burn up in the ozone or something.

Amma might surprise you, Tasneem said.

Anjali had surprised them both.

In the end, administration officials would only stay David's deportation on one condition.

He's going to be your brother, Anjali said.

Tasneem's eyes widened. You adopted him?

Essentially, yes, Anjali said. David? Is that okay with you?

Do I get to keep my compartment?

Not exactly, Anjali answered. Yours is larger than ours, so we will be moving into it with you. I'll be giving up the compartment that Tasneem and I share now.

Do I have to call you Mother?

You can call me Anjali, she replied.

David looked dubious.

Tasneem looked horrified.

Anjali knelt before the children. My dears, she said. This is a delicate situation. David, you understand that you were very close to being returned to Earth, yes?

David nodded.

And Tasneem, you have no desire to see your friend sent

away, yes?

Tasneem shook her head.

Then this solution is the only one, Anjali said. But David, you do not have to alter your life for us. I do not intend to mother you. You are clearly capable of managing your own affairs. I will be your mother if you like, but for now, I will just be your mother in the database. Do you understand?

You'll be my mother in name only, David said.

Do you agree? Anjali asked.

David looked past her at the open office she'd come from, and the shadowy men within.

I agree, he said.

Oh, boy, Tasneem said.

David turned to Tasneem. Wait until Audra finds out.

Anjali smiled at her daughter. My dear. Are you unhappy with this?

Tasneem looked up at her mother. I'm happy, she said.

Good, said Anjali. Now I shall take both of my children -- my real child and my fake child -- out for scoops of ice cream.

I like ice cream, David said.

Tasneem pressed her hands against her face.

Two Rivers

Follow these instructions.

Tasneem had ditched Blair. He wasn't surprised. She felt like an asshole, but he claimed to understand.

She gets off at juncture three, closing her eyes as she drops into the near-weightlessness of the disembarkment track. Blair stays on board, and is out of sight before she can offer even a final wave.

It doesn't matter.

Follow these instructions.

She had listened to the rest of the message enough times to memorize David's directions.

Go into your apartment, into the bathroom. Not the one in the main hall. The one attached to your sleeping quarters.

Her private bathroom. The one nobody entered but her.

The second light panel in your shower pod. Press the corners to unlatch it. You'll know what you're looking for when you see it. But since I'm dead, I probably shouldn't be vague here. You'll see a wristband, just like the old ones we used on Ganymede. Put it on and activate it with these words.

She tries not to imagine how David had discovered a secret panel in her own apartment. She doesn't even know of any.

River in heaven.

The words catch her off-guard on the first listen. Doctor Widla had said the same thing to her, hadn't he.

Your name. It means river in heaven. Rivers are like thread. They stitch things together.

She practically runs home.

She has never entered her apartment cautiously, but she does now. The light panels illuminate softly as she closes the door. For the first time, her home feels strange, as if it is not her own. As if someone has been here.

David? she calls.

There is no answer, but she does not feel foolish.

She had seen his body.

David was dead.

She walks on her toes, quietly.

David? she repeats.

Nothing.

David?

Oh, Tasneem.
David, what --
Tasneem, it's bad. It's so bad. I'm so sorry.
What? What happened? Are you okay? Are you --
Tasneem, it's your mother. Anjali.
My -- no. What happened?
Tasneem. Tasneem, Tasneem.
David! David, what happened?
Anjali is dead, Tasneem. She's dead. She's dead.
Wh -- Dav -- please. Don't lie. You're lying, you're lying.
No, Tasneem. No, no, no.

The memory rushes in.

David? she calls again.

The memory is so rich with his expression, the smell of his panic, that she cannot help but remember it so clearly.

It was the worst of times.

Her mother had died, Tasneem was certain, of the most awful loneliness. She knew that it had nothing to do with her, nothing to do with David's presence. Her mother desperately missed her father.

For years, her mother had talked to her father each morning. Tasneem would walk in on her mother, and ask what Anjali was doing.

Anjali would say, I'm telling your father about you and me.

And Tasneem would join her.

But as Tasneem grew up, she talked to her father less and less. She had never known him. But Anjali talked more, and over time she would emerge from her quarters later and later. In the past few weeks, Tasneem had not seen her mother before two p.m.

She frequently heard her crying softly.

People die of broken hearts, don't they? Tasneem had asked David.

Maybe, David had answered. It's not a scientific thing. It's one of those intangible things where human emotion affects human wellness. I think it' possible.

I think my mother died of hers, Tasneem had confided.

Things immediately changed.

Audra, who had resisted David's absorption into the Kyoh family, now insisted on sleeping over, convinced that Tasneem and David would fall in love by proximity alone. But both children grieved, and barely noticed Audra's behavior.

Station Administration officials arrived two days after Anjali's cremation.

Married? Tasneem had asked. But he's my adopted brother.

David sat beside her silently.

The first official said, The adoption is nullified in the event of the death of the adoptive parents.

In this case, there is only one parent, the second official said. And David is now essentially on the deportation list again.

Listen, the first official said, leaning forward. We are deeply sorry about this. We really don't have a choice.

There's just one solution to David's situation now, and it's what we've just explained, said the second official.

You want me to marry David, Tasneem repeated.

David still said nothing.

Ganymede law permits consenting juveniles to marry at the age of twelve, the first official explained. Tasneem, as a certified resident of the station, you are able to extend that status to David --

-- if the two of you are married, finished the second official.

We're twelve years old, Tasneem said.

Ganymede law permits consenting --

She heard you, David said.

The four of them sat silently in the compartment.

Finally, Tasneem said, If we didn't marry, David would be sent to Earth?

The first official nodded.

David would be deported by Sunday, the second official said.

But if I marry him --

Then David becomes a certified resident.

Tasneem nodded. She turned to David, who looked up at her balefully.

You don't have to, David said.

Tasneem turned to the administrators. If we do this -- does it have to be real? I mean, how does it work?

They had kept the secret their entire lives. Audra believed that David was simply allergic to the concept of marriage, and had stopped pressing her case in her twenties. They had cohabitated as partners ever since. She never knew that he had already been married for a decade to her best friend.

Audra, Tasneem thinks.

Audra had not changed much since childhood. She was a source of deep consternation to both Tasneem and David, but they both loved her, and accepted her.

And now she was committed to an institution, five-and-a-half months pregnant.

Oh, my, Tasneem thinks. What of the child?

Tasneem stands in the doorway of her sleeping quarters. She can almost feel David here, as if he had just been here moments ago.

David, she says once more.

Follow my instructions.

River in heaven.

The light panel detaches just as he had described. Tasneem lifts the panel and sets it aside. Exposed now is a slim depression in the wall. It's just enough space for the guts of the light panel to dwell.

But at the bottom of the depression there's a tiny shelf that the light panel rests upon.

And sitting on the shelf is a vintage wristband. It looks exactly like the one she owned when she was a child. She hasn't worn one in years.

River in heaven.

Tasneem puts the band on her left wrist. It fits well.

She presses and holds the center of the band, and it immediately syncs to her aural chip.

The band speaks into her ear.

Activate or erase?

Activate, Tasneem says.

The band issues two soft tones.

River in heaven, Tasneem says.

The band issues a positive tone, and then there is silence.

Tasneem looks down at the band, then sighs.

And then the voice speaks into her ear.

You found me.

Tasneem faints.

SOMA

Tasneem pours a cup of tea and takes it to the window. The apartment is dark, and outside, the concourse is mostly empty. She has found that the station adheres to Earth-time in most instances, setting appointments for morning or afternoon, unofficially observing the nighttime hours for sleep and the daytime hours for activity. But like any great city, there are night owls. She watches a few of them stroll along, lost in their own small worlds, giving each other the tiniest acknowledgment and continuing along their way.

She blows on her tea and waits for it to cool.

Finally she says, Okay. I think I'm ready.

Silence, and then:

I'm very sorry for the shock.

Though she was expecting it, the sound of David's voice in her ear -- practically in her head -- still finds her unprepared, and she almost drops her cup of tea. The cup rattles in her hands, which -- yes, she confirms it -- are actually shaking.

She exhales slowly, then inhales slowly. She repeats this a few times.

When she is calm, she says, This isn't real.

And David says, *But it is real, Tasneem.*

Jesus, she says, hopping out of her seat and backing away from the window. How are you doing that? *Who is doing that?*

Tasneem. Tasneem, calm. Breathe.

It is what David would say.

She breathes, and she says, I need proof.

Of course you do, David says. *I would be disappointed otherwise.*

How do I know you aren't some asshole reporter camped out somewhere with a remote wave system and a voice modulator?

You don't, not yet, David says. *Although I think you just made those two things up.*

Despite herself, she almost laughs.

David chuckles, too.

Alright. Tell me something that --

-- that only I could know? Sure. Where should I begin? Oh, I know. You once kissed me. You thought that I didn't know, but I knew. You thought that I was asleep. You couldn't have known that it takes me a very long time to fall asleep. I used to practice my breathing to try to lull myself into sleep. That's what I was doing when you crept over and kissed me. You know, it probably should have been unsettling, but it wasn't. Do you want to know something else, Tasneem?

Tears are streaming down Tasneem's face.

That was my first kiss, Tasneem. You would have thought Audra would have been the first, but it was you.

Oh, David, Tasneem says. I wish I could hug you.

Imagine it, David says. *Imagine it right now, quickly.*

Tasneem closes her eyes and imagines David standing in front of her. She enfolds him and squeezes tightly. God, I wish this was real, she says.

That was nice, David says. *Maybe the closest thing to physical contact I can enjoy now.*

You felt that?

I can read your biorhythms, actually. I can extrapolate emotion from a rise in adrenaline, or a rush of endorphins, and the context in which that change occurs.

David, I --

You're confused. I know. Why don't you sit, have some tea. I'll try to explain. It's simple, really.

Tasneem returns to the window. Her tea is still warm enough to drink. She folds one leg beneath her, then looks across the table at an empty chair.

She laughs.

What is it?

I just realized, Tasneem says, that I don't know where to look when you talk to me.

Would you say that I am a well-prepared man?

Tasneem says, Sure. You always have been.

And would you say I have the talent of observing possible outcomes, and responding to them?

Yes. What are you trying to say?

Have I ever done a rash thing in my life?

I can't think of anything, Tasneem says.

Then answer me this: if you were me, and you were going to have the treatment done, what would you do beforehand?

Tasneem considers this. I'd research the treatment carefully.

I did that. But that's not what I mean.

I'd choose the doctor carefully, she says. I'd learn about the interviews, and prepare for them.

I did not do those things, David says, *but then, I couldn't.*

Why, David?

Later, David says. *That's another topic altogether. But let's assume that, if I could have, I would have done those things. If you had been me, and you knew everything you could possibly know about the treatment -- what else would you have done?*

I suppose I would have said my goodbyes, she says. Just in case.

That's not it, either, David says.

Okay, then I give, David. I don't know what you're talking about.

As she says the words, she realizes that she is slipping back into easy conversation with him. Almost as if he hasn't actually gone anywhere. As if he's right here.

A good scientist always --

-- saves his work, Tasneem says. Okay, but --

Think about it.

It dawns on her a moment later. Holy shit, she says. It's not possible. David, that's just not possible.

But you're talking to me now, Tasneem. So it must be.

You backed -- you backed *yourself* up? They've been trying to do that for -- for decades!

Why risk nearly thirty-five years of careful study and work?

But David, it's not possible, it's just not. It can't be --

-- done? Oh, sure it can. In fact, it's been possible for nearly fifteen

years. But very few people know that, and almost nobody talks about it. It can be done, Tasneem, and I know that because I helped design the system that does it.

She doesn't know what to say.

Do you remember all those years on Ganymede? All those station line journeys to the college?

Well, yes. Of course I do.

Did you ever wonder what I was doing?

Tasneem smiles. Actually, I always had this sort of Biblical image of you. You were like the child Jesus, schooling the church elders. Except in this case, they were professors.

You're almost right, he says.

So you made a copy of yourself.

Yes.

How does that work?

It's complicated. But I designed a compression algorithm, and then I discovered that there were a few more tweaks that I could make, and so I made them, and then my little algorithm could suddenly take very, very, very big things and make them incredibly small. The human brain holds a massive amount of data, Tasneem. But all of those volumes of information -- well, they can fit onto a single chip, one so small you can't even see it.

Are you the first person to do this?

The first non-trial? Yes, I am. As far as I know, nobody else has died and lived on in an antique wristband.

This is amazing, David. She rearranges herself, then comes to a sudden realization. We have to tell Audra!

No, David says. *Nobody else can know, Tasneem. Nobody.*

But David, she's so --

Nobody. I love Audra to death, you know I do. But she cannot know about this.

Tasneem looks away.

Tasneem, David warns. *Promise me.*

I don't think I can, she says.

Promise me.

David --

Tasneem, promise me. I have my reasons. My reasons are never frivolous. Trust me.

She hesitates, then agrees. Alright. But David, what will she do? She's alone, she's pregnant, and -- David, they've committed her.

I know.

How do you know?

You didn't think that the only system hack I ever did was the one that invented my parents, did you?

I guess I never thought about it.

I'm connected to everything, Tasneem. I'm untraceable, I'm embedded in the station architecture, and I have the means to help us find something very special.

What do you mean, find something?

I think I can find a new home for us, David says.

I like my apartment just fine, Tasneem says.

That's not what I mean, David says. *I think that I can find us a new Earth.*

A new -- David.

I've been working on it for three years, he says. *Do you understand why it was important for me to create a backup of myself? Think of the lost data if I hadn't.*

I was too busy thinking about my lost friend, Tasneem says. It didn't even occur to me to think about this.

That's okay. That's why nobody will find me now. Nobody had any inkling that I could do this.

David, Tasneem says. What happens now?

What happens now is -- well, I don't know. We should talk about that.

How do I turn you off?

What do you mean?

I mean -- well, David, I have to pee. How do I turn you off?

Oh. Of course. Just remove the wristband.

Okay. I'll be right --

Tasneem. Listen, though. Once you remove it, you won't be able to hear me. And here's the thing -- right now, there's just one existing copy of my self, and it's on that band. If you lost it -- I'd be gone forever.

Tasneem looks down at the wristband. Then I guess I won't lose it.

Me. You won't lose me.

Right. You.

Tasneem?

Yes.

We should do something for Audra. But I don't know what. You're better at this sort of thing than I am.

Tasneem nods to herself. Let me think about it. We'll come up with something.

Tasneem sleeps poorly. At three, she gives up, and sits in the window again. The concourse is not dead -- there is a small knot of people who seem to be dancing, then talking among themselves, then dancing again.

What do you think they're doing?

I don't know. It looks like a club, maybe.

I suppose that's possible. Maybe a class.

Wait, Tasneem says. You see them.

There's no limit to my wonderful talents.

I don't understand. I keep saying that, but there are so many things.

It's not that complicated, David says. *I can read more than your biorhythms. I process information as if I'm a part of you. So while I don't have eyes, I can, essentially, see what you see.*

Tasneem keeps watching the dancers. That sounds suspiciously like you're reading my thoughts, she says.

That's pretty much what it is. Does that bother you?

She considers this. It should, you'd think. But I don't think it does.

Good.

David, she says.

Yes.

Tomorrow I'm having the Soma treatment.

I know.

I'm a little frightened.

You shouldn't be. It's not painful, I've heard.

I keep remembering -- you. How you looked.

That was different. Don't remember that.

I can't help it.

Soma is easy. A few transference patches, two days of observation, and you're as good as forever.

The doctor said something to me. Something about why I was having the treatment done.

What was it?

He told me it was because of my father.

Was he right?

I haven't been able to stop thinking of it. He said that my father died without knowing me. That he missed out. That it makes perfect sense for me to take Soma, because I don't want to miss out on anything.

It's a reasonable deduction. Do you think it's accurate?

I don't know. I don't want to miss out on anything, though. He's right about that. I was fortunate enough to be there when we left Earth and came to Ganymede. I've been here for Cassiopeia and Aries. I hear they're almost finished with Galileo.

Just another six or seven years, yes.

Right. But what comes next? What happens when we run out of space? We can't build space stations forever. Eventually we'll run out of room.

They'll build them to orbit the moon, maybe.

Okay. Maybe. But they'll run out of room there, too. So where do we go next? We can't go back to Earth.

I have some ideas about that.

See? Look at you, for instance. David, you're practically a god right now. You'll never die. Right? You are *forever*.

But I'm a crippled god, if that's what I am. I rely on you. No -- not crippled. I'm a parasitic god. If not for my host, I am nothing.

But what I mean is, you could last forever. In theory. Whether it's with me or not. And you'll be able to witness where our species is going. It's such a fascinating idea, David!

Will we build space stations around every planet? Will someone want to tunnel into the moon and build a hidden city?

Maybe they'll terraform Mars, David offers.

Exactly! It doesn't matter what it is -- I want to see it happen. I want to study our motivations. I want to understand our reasons.

What if we just self-destruct instead?

We've come together to build these stations, Tasneem says. I think we might have a little longer before that happens.

So you're not going to cancel your treatment, then.

Well, I never really considered canceling it. I was just nervous.

And what of Audra? What of her, while we live forever? What of my child?

I have a thought about that, David. Tell me what you think about this.

The outline of America has changed. Most of Florida is underwater. The bridge connecting North and South America is gone. South America looks like a slice of pie, half-eaten and surrounded by crumbs. There's a dramatic storm obscuring Canada.

It's very different, almost every day, Tasneem says.

Doctor Widla nods. Sometimes I watch it and I can almost imagine that I am seeing all of the land drowning, as if it's happening right there before me. Of course, it will be many centuries before that could happen. But can you imagine what it might look like? To look down on a great blue ocean planet?

It would be a thing of great beauty, Tasneem says.

And great sadness, Dr. Widla agrees.

You could see it, Tasneem says. If the space stations are still here then.

I'm sure the space stations will be here for many centuries to come. But I will not.

Tasneem is surprised. What do you mean? Surely you've had --

Soma? Dr. Widla shakes his head. No, I haven't.

But why not?

I am a lonely man, Tasneem, he says. I had a wife, once. I miss her every day. I could not bear that for centuries more. Even a decade seems unpleasant to consider.

My mother was like you, Tasneem says. It was bad enough when my father died, but she hung on. I think when we moved to Ganymede, she felt like her grasp of him had been severed. She lasted for as long as she could.

I would have liked to meet her, Dr. Widla says.

The two of them stand at the window, watching the Earth gently turn.

David whispers in her ear. *I didn't ask you before, but -- would you keep me on your wrist? During?*

Tasneem doesn't answer, but she doesn't have to.

Doctor Widla places his hand on Tasneem's shoulder. She looks up at his kind face.

Well, my dear, he says. Let's begin.

The Settlers

BLAIR

These two casualties bring the total number to twenty-seven.

Unbelievable, Stanley.

It certainly is, Lisa.

On that note, let's take a look at preparations for the Cosmo Bowl this Saturday...

Bullshit. It's bullshit, Tamara, and you know it's --

Blair, Jesus, yes, I know, I get it. You're not screen talent, though. It's the same old argument I have with you and every other pulse writer. I want to be on camera, let me be on camera, why didn't you let me be on camera?

Blair turns and slams his fist against the door. I'm not every other writer, Tamara, and you know it.

Tamara Antelo sighs. You're right. But you're also not screen-ready, Blair. I don't know how else to tell you.

Blair flops into the chair opposite Tamara's desk. I feel like a drama queen, he mutters.

You and every other reporter have played that same part for about a hundred and fifty years. You're no more dramatic than the rest of them.

It's just -- you know I've been chewing on this story for months now. I deserve the credit for it.

Tamara opens her arms. That's not how it works, Blair. You want credit, go independent. You want visibility, stay here. You'll get a shot, but not before you're ready.

Twenty-seven people are dead, Tamara. From a medical treatment that's, you know, supposed to make you live forever. I've done a lot of legwork on this. I've talked to a lot of people. I've seen David Dewbury's bloated corpse. The least you can do is let me talk about it on screen. Let Stanley fucking interview me -- I don't care. I don't need to be the face of the studio. But the words should come out of my mouth, one way or another.

You're stubborn, Tamara says. It's not very original, but it works. So I'll tell you this -- you get me an exclusive to go along with all of that hard work, something I can promo the shit out of, and I'll... I'll put you on screen. Stanley will ask the questions, you can be the expert. Fair enough?

Done, Blair says.

Alright. Get the hell out of my space.

He won't see you, Mr. Hudgens. Not after last time.

Come on, Blair says. Look, it's not his fault. He didn't

invent the stuff, he just administers it.

Doctor Widla was shredded on screenview, Mr. Hudgens. The entire fleet saw it. He had to let the whole staff go.

Except you, I see.

Somebody's got to answer when slugs like you call. Goodbye.

Fuck, Blair says. He leans his head back against the fast-track window.

Six years following Dewbury's death from Amrita, the black-market version of Soma, the story had turned. Soma patients themselves were beginning to die -- they just toppled over on the concourse, never got out of bed, slumped over their breakfasts. Nobody was sure yet what was happening -- when they were, Blair hoped to be right there to get the details. It was almost as if a switch in their brains was flipped. They just... went dark. Some survived for a few days in a comatose state, but most were dead on the spot.

Nearly one hundred Soma treatments had been performed successfully so far.

Twenty-seven of those patients were dead within nine months of undergoing treatment.

Doctor Widla and two other specialists in the fleet were the only professionals authorized to administer Soma. Doctors Frank Hart and Amelie Golding weren't talking, either. Blair had heard that Dr. Golding had attempted suicide, but had been found in time. He couldn't get a confirmation on the story yet.

The doctors wouldn't talk. He couldn't get a full list of Soma patients.

He's running out of people to talk to.

And then it comes to him.

I feel like an idiot for not thinking of you sooner, he says.

I don't think I can offer much, says Tasneem. I already know what you're going to ask me. And no, I'm not dead.

Blair laughs. You never called me back after your deposition.

Ah, I see what this is about now, Tasneem says. I'm sorry. Something came up, and I got very distracted.

I won't ask, he says. He smiles. It's really very nice to see you.

I have an idea of what you want, she says. I'm not wild about the idea, but I have a feeling it will be good for you.

It will help me get on screen, he says. You'll do an interview?

I'm not sure why anybody will care, Tasneem answers. I'm not a celebrity.

Trust me, Blair says. People are going to care. They're going to care a lot.

Stanley Wilk raises his eyebrow. Did you expect me to complain?

Tamara nods. Actually, I did. You're not following the plot.

The plot sucks. He's a good kid. Give him the break.

You're sure? I want you to be sure.

I'm sure.

We'll cut to him after twelve, then, Tamara says. Can you set him up?

I'll wing it.

You think he'll do alright?

Stanley shrugs. What do I know? I've never seen him on screen. But he's smart. He'll probably be fine. Make sure he has a drink before he goes on. First interviews are always jittery.

I should send him on screen drunk? Tamara asks.

Not drunk. Bright. He'll be smoother.

This sounds like a trade secret I'd rather not know, Stanley.

Stanley bends forward. Then I would advise staying out of Lisa's dressing quarters.

You look nice today.

Thank you.

Are you nervous?

I don't know. Should I be?

I don't know.

Are you?

I don't know.

Do you think this is going to go well?

For you? Or for me?

I don't know. For both of us.

It will go well.

I hope so.

Just remember -- it's only a conversation.

You and me.

Right. You and me.

Okay.

I think they're ready for us.

Okay.

Are you okay?

I can't tell.

Let's go.

Okay.

You underwent Soma, what -- five years ago?

Six, Tasneem says.

She is sitting in a bowl-shaped chair, knees carefully crossed. She rests her hands on her thighs and tries to keep breathing smoothly.

Six years, Blair says.

He's a natural, she thinks. He leans back just a bit, then finds his way forward when asking more intimate questions, as if bringing himself into the story itself.

Offscreen, Tamara is thinking the same thing.

Six years, Blair repeats. And tell me, did you know any of the Soma patients who have unfortunately passed away?

I didn't, Tasneem says. Actually, I don't know any Soma

patients personally. There aren't so many of us, you know.

And Soma is administered on all three stations now, Blair adds, which makes it a little harder to meet, I presume.

I'm sure, Tasneem says.

I want to ask you a question, and I hope you'll answer it honestly, Blair says, leaning forward a tiny bit.

Of course, Tasneem says. I'll try.

Blair sets his jaw and softens his eyes. Are you scared?

Tasneem slows her breathing, hesitates.

Blair waits patiently.

I --

It's okay, he says when Tasneem falters a little.

Tasneem exhales slowly. Yes. Of course, I'm scared. With the news, I'm not sure anybody wouldn't be.

What does it feel like, knowing that death may be coming?

She closes her eyes. It feels... hollow. Inevitable.

But so far, you've been lucky, Blair says.

Very, she answers, opening her eyes.

Do you feel cheated?

Cheated?

You underwent months of psychiatric evaluation, of painful investigation of your past, for a treatment that is designed to extend your life by as long as one hundred years, Blair says. With Soma, your life expectancy of one hundred years just became two hundred. And that's just speculation, because nobody knows how effective the treatment will be at such distant points in the future. So, yes, that's my question -- do you feel cheated?

Tasneem shakes her head. I don't know. I hadn't thought about it in quite that way. I suppose it's possible, but for now,

I'm alive. Ask me again when I'm dead?

Blair laughs. Well, let me ask you about that streak in your hair, then.

Oh, this, Tasneem says, fingering the white stripe in her otherwise dark hair.

So far, the patients who have died from Soma have reportedly witnessed their own hair go white before they passed away, Blair says. What does that white stripe mean to you?

Tasneem looks up at the lock of white hair that she's holding away from her face. It means, so far, that I'm a survivor.

I wonder if perhaps, to you, it symbolizes the approach of your own mortality, or would you characterize it more as the souvenir of a brush with death?

Tasneem considers this. I can't say, really. This happened about a month ago. How soon after their hair went white did the other patients die?

Most were within days, Blair says.

Perhaps I'm a lucky survivor, then, Tasneem says.

Is there anything about you that might have countered the treatment's horrible side effect? Perhaps something about your lifestyle?

I practice yoga, Tasneem says. I don't drink.

No secret weapons, then, Blair says with a smile.

I can't think of any, she answers.

Let's assume the worst, Blair says. Let's assume that you leave here today, and you were to die tonight.

That's morbid, Tasneem says.

It is. But if that were the case -- would you want to share

any last words with the rest of mankind here, today?

Tasneem thinks about it. I don't think I have anything worth saying, she says. I'm not that eloquent.

Blair grins. Well, we will continue to hope for the best for you, Tasneem Kyoh. Thanks for being here today.

Afterward, Blair shakes her hand, then says, No kidding, is there something you're doing?

What do you mean? Tasneem asks.

The dead Soma patients were sheer white, he says. Hair, pure white. Yours seems to have stopped. I just can't help thinking of it as a sign that you're going to get through this. Like this stripe is your battle scar.

Maybe it is, Tasneem says.

They shake hands again, and he walks her to the lobby.

If anything happens -- anything at all, he says, will you call me?

I'll call you before I call my doctor, she says.

I don't mean to be selfish, Blair says. Really, I don't. But I think you may have just made my career tonight.

I'm glad, Blair. I hope so.

Be safe, Tasneem. Live forever.

I hope to, she says.

He watches her go, small and composed. Then he steps back into the studio, and heads for Tamara's office.

EMIL

STICKERS

Emil doesn't like this hospital.

There are seven on Station Aries. They wrap like a sleeve around the ring-shaped station, and rotate slowly as the days pass. Each of the patients' quarters has a beautiful view of Earth, though Earth is not so beautiful itself anymore. The patients can see the sun, and sometimes the moon, and they can watch the hurricanes that gnaw at the coastlines far below.

On a good day, they can see the lifeboats singing into the heavens like balls of light.

There are always enough beds.

But this hospital is a farce. It is the only one on Station Galileo, which is a hideous block that lumbers around the Earth now.

He thinks back on the stations. Ganymede, the first, was designed for function and immediacy, and was based on the lessons learned by NASA and Roscosmos and others. It was expected to be full of cables and exposed guts, and it was. Over the years, Ganymede's residents have renovated the station, turning it into a glowing filament of life. He hears that Ganymede is the station most visible from Earth.

Cassiopeia was not much better to begin with, and has not improved with time. He hears it described as a shopping mall, an industrial park. It is a complex stack of cubes and corridors, where people are often lost.

And Aries -- home sweet Aries -- is the fleet's golden star, a series of rings that spin and turn like Saturn. Most refugees from the planet below request asylum on Aries. It is a technological hub, though it was not designed as such. It has emerged as a home for science, while Cassiopeia has developed a reputation as a home for believers.

Everyone had expected that Galileo, named for one of the great astronomers, would trump them all.

Instead, the entire station looked like a school cafeteria.

Its hospital was no better.

Windowless.

Bland.

The corridors were infinitely long. The floor, ceiling and walls were all the same interminable shade of beige, so that it was not difficult to lose track of yourself as you walked. The smell of iodine hung in the air, as if doctors were conducting business on a Civil War battlefield instead of in a floating hospital in space.

Perhaps that is what bothers Emil most.

This is space, goddammit. Why does it feel like a shipping container at the bottom of the sea?

He picks up his coffee cup and abandons his table in the physician's lounge, taking his screenview with him. He often uses it to watch the public video feeds broadcast from the Aries. There's one external camera on that space station that isn't too far from his own office, and watching the slow pinwheel of Earth past the station reminds him just a little bit of home.

He dumps the coffee out and throws away the cup, tucking the screenview beneath his arm.

At he door, he pauses.

What is that infernal buzzing? he asks.

There is one other doctor in the lounge. She glances up at him, frowns, and then looks up at the lights.

He follows her gaze to the ceiling, where fluorescent bulbs hum behind textured plastic covers.

You're shitting me, he says.

The other doctor shakes her head. I do not shit you, she says.

Emil yanks the door open. It's like they time-traveled to the 1980s to build this place, he grumbles.

The other doctor returns to her crossword. 1970s, maybe, she says.

Emil smiles despite himself. Hey, he says.

The doctor looks up.

I'm Emil Widla, he says.

I know, she says. Soma guy. Don't envy you.

He stares, waiting for her name, but she doesn't offer it.

So he leaves.

Seventy-six Soma patients are dead.

The treatments were finally banned when the mortality count hit fifty, which meant that nearly two hundred people were given Soma before the wall came down. One hundred eighty-five, actually. This befuddled Emil. While Soma patients were already dying, there were still people lining up for treatment, and new doctors emerging who were quite willing to administer it.

Frank Hart and Amelie Golding, the other two physicians licensed for Soma treatment, were both dead now.

Golding had attempted suicide twice, and had been resuscitated both times. Emil had actually been on his way to visit her when she finally managed to finish the job. He guesses that when you fail at the easy way -- both of her prior attempts had involved medications -- you gain the nerve to go out hard.

She had cut her own throat.

Frank had gone into hiding when he and his family started receiving death threats. He turned up underneath one of the station cars on Ganymede. Nobody saw anything, and he had been labeled a suicide as well. Emil suspected otherwise, but had troubles of his own. He wasn't unfamiliar with death threats, either. Maybe he was spared because he was trying to treat the victims when nobody else was.

Of the remaining one hundred nine patients, forty have agreed to come to Galileo for observation and medical attention. The sixty-nine left refused to spend their unknown number of final days within Galileo's walls, and Emil cannot blame them. If at any moment you might die, better to spend those precious minutes with family, or space-diving from Aries' inner ring.

But here he is now, with a meager support staff and little patience for the daily media requests that pile up on his desk.

He walks slowly down Corridor 7, where most of the forty have been sequestered from the rest of the hospital. It is eerily silent here. General hospital staff are not permitted. While the corridor is not quarantined, it may as well be. Patients are not permitted visitors. Emil thinks this is probably the reason most Soma patients refused to participate.

Who wants to spend their last days forcibly removed from their loved ones?

So the forty are a strange bunch. Most are isolationists and introverts. Most are very, very wealthy. Soma is not the most affordable treatment on the market. Well, that's not true. Before it was banned, the cost dropped dramatically, and people with little to lose signed up for what had become certain death.

And yet they hope.

They hope for a cure. They hope they are an exception. They hope for an asteroid to tear through the entire fleet, so that at least if they have to die, everybody else does, too.

Emil pauses beside the first room.

Nurse Lynne appears from nowhere.

Where did you come from? Emil asks.

From room 22, the nurse responds. Mr. Fitz is displeased with his room. Again.

Mr. Fitz is quite welcome to leave, Emil says. It is the only way he will find a room more to his liking.

Are you making rounds?

I'm about to, he answers. Why?

The nurses are in the office watching something, she says.

He takes the screenview she offers him. What is it? he asks.

She touches the screen, and it begins to play.

The image is of a warmly-lit news studio. Two large chairs, shaped like deep bowls, stand unoccupied. Beyond the chairs -- Emil sighs at the image -- is large glass wall, through which Earth, in its haunted glory, hangs like a glowing coal.

Theme music plays, and two people enter and sit down in the bowls.

It's Tasneem, Emil says.

Nurse Lynne nods. Yes.

And that man -- he's familiar.

His name is Blair Hudgens, Doctor. He's been pestering the office for a chance to interview you for months.

Ah, Emil says. Let's watch, let's watch.

Did you know any of the Soma patients who have unfortunately passed away?

Actually, I don't know any Soma patients personally.

Emil frowns. Her hair, he says. It's white! But -- it's only a little bit. A stripe, almost.

I think it's pretty, the nurse says.

Emil shoots the nurse a hard look. White means death, he

says.

Not for her, she says.

He pinches his eyes shut. What do you mean, not for her?

Here, the nurse says.

She advances the video.

Watch this, she says.

Let me ask you about that streak in your hair, then.

Oh, this?

Patients who have died from Soma have witnessed their own hair go white before they died. What does that white stripe in your hair mean to you?

That I'm a survivor, I guess.

Would you characterize it as the souvenir of a brush with death?

This happened about a month ago. How soon after their hair turned white did the other patients die?

Most within days.

Perhaps I'm a survivor, then.

Emil turns to the nurse in surprise. How long ago was this? This interview?

The nurse says, I don't know. I think it was last month.

And nobody told me until now? Emil says. Why not?

I -- we didn't know, the nurse says.

Well, we must have her, Emil says. Go! Find her. Bring Tasneem here as fast as you can.

I don't know --

You don't know, you don't know, Emil says. No excuses! She may be our answer. Find her as quickly -- and as quietly! -- as you can.

The nurse nods. Yes, Doctor.

Oh, Emil says.

Nurse Lynne stops in her tracks. Yes?

Tell Mr. Fitz that another patient has died. That will ease his bitching.

Doctor, the nurse says. That's awful. I won't lie to him.

Oh, you're not lying, Emil says. Another has.

I didn't hear about anyone, the nurse says. Who was it?

Mrs. Ross, Emil says. I'm sorry I forgot to mention it.

Poor Mrs. Ross, Nurse Lynne says. Alright. I'll tell him.

If he complains again, put him out an airlock, Emil says.

The nurse clucks and trots away.

Emil hesitates outside the first door.

He doesn't want to open it.

Nurse Lynne, he says, but she has already disappeared around the corner.

Nurse Lynne, he says again.

When there is no response, he sighs and continues walking.

The corridor connects to a shorter one, which leads to another one, which leads to the nurses' office. It's difficult to stage anything resembling a central brain in this hospital -- another reason he despises the place. Nurses and doctors should operate from the center, and radiate outward to reach all of their patients quickly and efficiently, he thinks.

Here, though, doctors must run and slide around corners and crash into walls and run again and get lost in the haze of beige, beige, beige everywhere.

He passes six patient rooms. Each door is closed, except for the last.

Room 17 stands open.

Emil pauses at the door and peeks inside.

Miss Gretchen, he says.

The room is empty.

Like each of the patient rooms, it is sparsely furnished. The bed has a hood that can be lowered to isolate the patient. There is a simple table beside the bed. A screenview rests on the table. There's a stool for visitors. Not a chair -- a stool. The room is beige, just like the rest of the hospital, but absent any windows.

The room feels like a sac puffed full of stale air.

Miss Gretchen, he says again.

He leaves and walks to the nurses' office. The office is surprisingly quiet. Nurse Lynne is there, speaking into her screenview. He doesn't recognize the face speaking back to her.

Nurse Allen is there, too.

Nurse, he says. Where is Miss Gretchen?

Nurse Allen glances up. Miss Gretchen, she says. Miss

Gretchen.

In Room 17, he says.

Right, okay. Room 17. I -- she shouldn't be anywhere. I don't know what -- is she not in her room?

She's not in her room, he says. Go find her.

Emil steps aside and the nurse hurries by.

He enters the office and takes a seat behind Nurse Lynne. A crude chart is spread out on the table before him, mapping the forty occupied rooms. Each room has small, colored sticker on it.

Emil picks up the chart and studies it.

Room 1, black sticker.

Room 2, red sticker.

Rooms 3 through 6, black stickers.

He scans ahead.

Room 17.

White sticker.

Black stickers mean *present*. You're a Soma patient. You're probably going to die. You're here.

Red stickers mean *dead*. There have been three of these already.

White stickers.

White stickers mean *any moment now*.

White stickers mean your hair has gone white.

White stickers mean you're on watch.

White stickers don't stay white for very long.

He looks over the rest of the chart.

Every red sticker is applied on top of a white one.

White stickers mean you're about to get a red sticker.

Emil sighs and drops the chart. He leans back in the chair

and runs his hands through his thinning hair.
Nurse Lynne is still talking to a stranger.
Emil wishes he had never heard of Soma.

GRETCHEN

She refuses to meet with him in her room.

Emil meets her in the physician's lounge. She's there when he arrives.

Before he enters, he turns to Nurse Lynne. No one comes in, he says.

Nurse Lynne nods, then pushes the door open for him.

Miss Gretchen is sitting at one of the tables. She looks up when he enters. Her hair is brilliant white. Her eyes appear even darker in contrast. She smiles at him, and he feels his heart sink.

It's always hardest when they smile.

Miss Gretchen, he says.

She stands up, and he takes her hands.

She smiles.

I'm sorry that this is the only room we have, he says.

Gretchen shakes her head. It's okay, she says. I won't --

I know, he says. I understand.

I won't die in that room, she says. I just won't.

I want to tell you that I'm sorry, he says.

Oh, Emil, she says. It isn't your fault. Don't burden yourself with that. How many is it now? A hundred? Two? That's too much burden for any man to carry. One is too much.

You're the first patient who ever called me Emil, he says.

They sit down together at the table.

I don't want to be a patient anymore, she says. So I'll be Gretchen, and you can be Emil. And none of this Miss bullshit anymore, either. Now that I have this hair, I certainly don't want to be made to feel older than I am.

Fair enough, says Emil.

So, she says. First things first. Will it hurt?

He presses his lips together, then chews one absently.

That's a nervous-making kind of non-answer, Gretchen says.

Emil smiles sadly. I'm sorry. Nervous habit, maybe. I can't really answer your question.

Gretchen nods. I know. Nobody sticks around long enough to talk to. I've read as much as I could.

Emil places his hands flat on the table. I wish that wasn't the case.

I don't know how I'm feeling right now, she says. I guess everyone probably thought they were going to be the exception. That they'd be the one person who didn't succumb to -- to whatever it is. I know I did.

It's human nature, he says.

I saw the interview, Gretchen says. The one with the woman you treated.

Emil sighs and closes his eyes. I wish you hadn't.

One of your nurses, she says. She thought it might give me hope.

Oh, it probably does, he says. And that's why I wish you

hadn't seen it. Which nurse?

Oh, I won't tell. You leave her -- him? -- alone. Gretchen smiles. I'm glad to have seen it. It means that maybe we can get around whatever this is.

You'd want that? Emil asks.

What do you mean?

I'd have thought this experience might have soured you on the idea of life extension treatment, he says. Some Soma patients became protesters when they learned what was happening. One tried to introduce legislation to ban it. He died before it was successful, but the cause carried on without him.

Oh, I don't want it banned, she says. I wish it wasn't. We have to learn from this, Emil. We have to solve it. Our lives are too fragile. If we're ever going to restore ourselves, we'll need more tenacity than we've got right now.

Tenacity, he says. That's a good word. We are kind of lacking in it, aren't we.

Gretchen looks around the room. As evidenced by our surroundings, she says. Is that fluorescent lighting?

God, Emil says. I'm glad someone else noticed.

The humming is going to kill me, Gretchen says. I've a good mind to die right now.

Please don't, Emil says. This is the most refreshing conversation I've had all day.

Well, that's tragic.

This place doesn't exactly inspire, does it, he says.

No, it does not, Gretchen says.

Emil puts his hands on the table. Gretchen, do you have anything better to do right now?

I have absolutely nothing planned, she says.

Would you like to take a walk with me? he asks.

I'd like nothing better, Emil.

Nurse Lynne knows a guy who knows a guy. A few hallways, sharp turns and unlocked doors later, Gretchen turns to Emil and says, breathlessly, This is not a bad place to go, you know what I mean?

Emil is deeply surprised to find that he agrees with her.

Galileo, for all of its drab interiors -- even its exterior feels like an interior -- has startled them both. Like a glass-bottomed boat, the space station has a viewport that rivals all of Aries.

Why is this closed? Gretchen asks.

But Emil can only shrug.

Nurse Lynne's friend's friend gives Emil a tiny salute, and pulls the access door closed behind him.

They are alone.

And yet.

The viewing deck is a long, wide room with a glass floor. Mounted to the walls are harnesses.

Emil wanders over to one and runs his fingers along the contraption.

No, Gretchen says. You think?

They aren't difficult to figure out, and Emil carefully straps Gretchen in. The shoulder harness clasps across her chest.

Her feet buckle flat against the wall, her knees bent.

When she is secure, he says, Are you ready?

Go slowly, she says.

She grips his hand.

He releases the tether line, letting it out a few inches at a time, until Gretchen says, Stop.

Emil locks the tether in place.

Gretchen is suspended a couple of feet above the floor, facing the glass.

Well, he says. Is it worth it?

You should join me and see, she says. But yes. Yes, it's very much worth it.

I'm not sure I can buckle myself in without help, he says. That tether required all of my strength.

Gee, thanks, Gretchen says, laughing.

Emil sits cross-legged on the floor beside her. It's a beautiful view, isn't it.

I certainly didn't expect it, Gretchen says. This station is like living inside of a cheese grater. Except there are fewer windows.

Emil chuckles.

Thank you, Gretchen says.

Are you scared?

I'm -- I'm not sure, she answers. Maybe? Maybe a little bit.

I don't know if it's painless, he says. But I've seen a few of these now, and they're fast.

Oh, don't tell me, please, she says.

Okay, Emil says.

They fall silent, taken in by the view. The sun is behind the Earth somewhere, and the planet seems to pulse with light. In the dark they can see the faintest glow of cities. There are fewer lights every day.

Do you remember Earth? she asks.

Emil nods. I'm a great deal older than you. Most of my life was lived down there.

Gretchen says, Do you ever miss it?

Perhaps. I miss what it was, maybe, he says. It's not the same place now.

He looks up at her. And you? Do you miss it?

Her eyes seem very far away.

I miss her, she says.

As the Earth slides beneath them, Gretchen tells Emil a story.

Her name was Molly, she says. We found each other in high school, just a few years before I moved to Cassiopeia with my sister and mother. That we found each other seems the best way to put it, though I don't think either of us knew we were searching for each other. I still remember the day that she saw me for the first time. That's how it happened. She saw me. I didn't see her.

Emil just listens.

I'd had a terrible fight with my mother that morning, Gretchen continues. I don't remember what it was about. That's how it always works, you know. You remember the fight, but you forget the reason for it. I had called my mother a horrible, terrible name. I'd been doing that a lot lately. I guess that day, Mother had had enough, and she told me that I was a bitch. She didn't mean it. We both knew that she didn't. After she said it, she got this horrified look on her face, and she started to cry. She came to me, trying to apologize, but I knew how much it would hurt her if I just ran, so that's what I did. I didn't give her the chance to make it right, even though I knew it wasn't really her fault.

Molly was new -- isn't that the way these stories always go? She was new, and she was nervous. My school was in Texas, in the part of Houston that hadn't been submerged yet. She was from somewhere inland. Minnesota, I think. Someplace that used to be cold, but wasn't anymore. And I never could figure out -- why would you move from safe ground to the new coast? Usually everybody was doing the opposite. I lost a lot of friends in those years. Most of them moved to places like Montana, where they were safe.

I lived in Montana, Emil says. Butte.

I've never been, Gretchen says.

Go on.

Molly saw me in the library, standing in a corner, just pressing my head against the brick. I used to do things like that to myself back then. Some girls would cut themselves, but me, I liked to find unconventional ways to hurt myself. The brick was pretty rough, and I wasn't, so when Molly came up and asked if I was okay, when I turned to look at her, there were these thin lines of blood coming out of my forehead and dripping down my face. What can I say? I was a dramatic child. But look, you can still see the rough patch on my forehead.

Emil tilts his head to see. Your hair is in the way.

Gretchen wiggles her arms. I'm pretty well immobilized here, she says.

Emil sweeps her hair back with his palm. Oh, yes. I see it. That must have hurt.

I don't remember. But Molly was unflappable. She just pulled a tissue from her bag and said, You probably know already, but you're bleeding a little. A little! I had blood on my shirt, my cheeks, my nose. And there she was with a tissue, this scared new girl who just -- she found me. And I started to cry, all snotted-out and gross.

What did Molly do? Emil asks.

She took me to the bathroom and she cleaned me up, Gretchen says. And that was sort of the beginning of what was going to be something wonderful.

Going to be?

Well, when you fall in love on a fucked-up planet, sometimes bad things happen at the wrong times, Gretchen says. Molly and I never got to so much as hold hands. We talked for hours in the library, and she told me about her favorite books, and I told her books were silly, and so she read some of her favorite parts to me. She liked this one book about Mars, it had all these little stories about people moving to Mars. I still read it every year, just to remember her a little.

It sounds familiar, Emil says.

You think? Gretchen says.

What happened to Molly?

She let me walk her home that afternoon. She didn't know the area yet. And we talked all the way there, and when we got to her building, she invited me to her room, and we talked until her father told me I had to go home so they could eat.

Sometimes I wish I had stayed, but I went home to my mother and my sister, and Molly sat down to eat dinner with her family, and they all died.

What was it?

The stupidest thing, Gretchen says. They were renting in one of the neighborhoods that was probably going to be next to go. You have to remember, in those days, the rain was practically constant, and a lot of places flooded, and a lot of buildings got insane amounts of water damage. And I guess what happened with their building was that there was a weak spot in the sub-basement, and nobody knew, but all of the rain had basically broken through, and for weeks the basement was just filling up with mud and water and sludge, and then a few things just gave out, and the whole apartment building just fell inward on itself.

She died, Emil says.

She died. So did her father, and whoever else was in her family. I didn't meet them all. Everybody else in the building died, too. That wasn't uncommon in those days. No survivors. Nobody to rescue. You remember how it was.

Well, I was in Montana. It was a little different there, Emil says. But I remember a lot of the coastal states stopped trying to pull people out when things like that were happening.

Yes, Gretchen says. It happened almost every day. Nobody can rescue that many people.

So you lost her, he says. What a tragedy. Do you think she felt --

The same way? Gretchen asks. I hope so. I don't know. I mean, I'm sure I've romanticized this memory of this one day. But she was the one. Do you know?

Emil nods. I know.

And I guess I've always been content to live without replacing her, Gretchen says.

Do you regret that now?

Gretchen considers this. You know, I don't think I do.

Good, Emil says. Regrets are hell.

You say that like a man who has a few, Gretchen says.

I don't know any men who don't, Emil says.

Tell me one, Gretchen says.

Emil shifts on the glass floor. I couldn't. What a waste of your last --

He stops. I'm sorry.

Don't be, Gretchen says. I've nothing to say, really. Tell me a story.

A story, Emil says.

Gretchen smiles. Tell me the last bedtime story I'll ever hear.

So he does.

ISONA

I am not so good at telling stories, but I will tell you this one.

When I was a boy, my father moved my family to America. It is funny to start my story like this. It sounds like a very old story, but it is not. I am not quite that old.

My father could build things. Applications and computers and such. Things I never learned, despite our home being a wreck of devices and our dinner conversation being about things like software platforms and databases. But he was an impatient man, and he didn't do his research, and he moved us to Montana instead of to California, where there were jobs for people like him.

He spent all of our money getting us to America, and then he didn't have enough to get us to California. He couldn't find a job doing what he loved to do, so he did what all parents do when they must. He took a job that meant nothing to him, and then took two more on top of that. He waited tables, and he carried luggage. And at night he continued to write programs. He was very tired all of the time, my father. I didn't see him very much.

When I was thirteen years old, my father created an application that would find a pen pal for you. He told me that he felt very bad that he was always busy, so he had made this application just for me, so that I might find some friends. I wasn't making friends in Montana. My accent was troublesome, and I thought that the children there were boring. They liked guns, and I liked books.

I didn't want to use this program that he made. I was angry with him, like boys are. I understand now what he was trying to do, but oh, what an ungrateful shit I was then.

But then he died.

He died in the stupidest way, and left me alone.

Remember, my father was tired all the time. He would sleep two or three hours at night, and then work, work, work. I know now that it was all to keep me in good clothes and stuffed with food, but at the time, I really didn't like him. He would come home from work, and he would go into the corner of our little apartment and keep working. And I would fall asleep in my sleeping bag listening to the clack, clack, clack of his computer keys. To this day, I hate that sound.

When I was thirteen I thought that my father was so in love with his work that he would work all day, then come home and work, work some more. I thought he loved it more than me. And he did love it, but not that much. I didn't understand that he would come home and try to build these applications that might make him a wealthy man.

He only wanted to give me opportunities. He was like any immigrant father in that respect.

I only gave him grief.

He died because he was tired. He woke at four in the

morning to go to work at one of his jobs -- he kept adding new ones and discarding other ones, and I don't know which one he was going to that morning. But he got up, dressed, kissed me goodbye, and drove to work on the wrong side of the road. He had forgotten, maybe, that he was in America. It was so early that there was almost nobody on the road, but still my father drove into them. And he died.

I was a petulant boy. When my father kissed me each morning, I was awake, but I would pretend to be asleep. I would hate the way his whiskers poked me. I would fill myself with anger until my body was so stiff that I woke up with cramps and old-man posture.

I wish I had kissed him back that day.

When he died, I was given to the state, and sent to live with several families, a different one every few months. None of them wanted to keep me. I was a very challenging foster child, I suppose. I was always closing myself away in rooms, always sticking my nose into books. I didn't sleep well, or often. I had nightmares. I cried an awful lot. It's not easy, I guess, for a family to adopt a teenager who is having a perpetual nervous breakdown.

So I was sent from one home to the next to the next. And one family had another little boy, and this little boy was a snoop and a jackass. All of my possessions in the world were inside a single box. One afternoon I returned home from school, and the contents of my box were strewn all over the house. I found my favorite book in the oven.

But that little boy did me the greatest favor of all.

Because one of the items in the box was my father's tablet computer. And the boy, this little bastard, he cracked the screen, and I was so upset. I was so overwhelmingly upset that I was shaking and unable to cry. I was full of regret then, remember, and so my father's computer was at once precious and anathema to me.

I turned it on to make sure that it was not broken, and it wasn't.

And there on the screen was the application that my father had made for me.

Gretchen says, Can you take me down from this harness?

Yes, Emil says. Are you okay?

Yes, I think so, Gretchen says. It's just that all the blood rushes to your face after a while.

Emil pulls the tether until Gretchen is upright, then releases her feet.

Ooh, she says. Tingly.

She stands up, knees a little shaky.

Emil sits back down.

Go on, Gretchen says. I'm just going to walk until my legs wake up right. What happened after that?

What happened was I started crying.

My father, he would always leave these little notes for me where only I would notice them. Like when we first moved to Montana, I saw this movie where these two people were in love, but one of them worked for an evil empire, and the other one was part of the rebellion. And all of these awful things happened between those two groups, but these two people, they would leave notes for each other in the form of symbols. A circle meant *I'm okay*. A circle with a dot in it was *I'm hurt*. Things like that.

And so my father would do things like that.

When the application loaded, there was a startup screen that was pretty crude. The app was called Pen Me. It was a play on words, right, but my father was always bad at English, so while the intention was good, it sort of didn't work all that well. But anyway, right there on the screen, in plain sight, was a little circle with three dots in it.

Three dots meant *I love you*.

So that's why I cried. My father was gone, but it was like he was my own pen pal from beyond the grave. That's heavy and melodramatic, maybe, but that's how it felt to me at thirteen.

Was the program any good? Gretchen asks.

She sits down next to Emil and rests her head on his shoulder. Her white hair bows into his face a little, but it smells nice, and he doesn't mind. He puts an arm around her without thinking.

Gretchen leans into him a little more. That's nice, she says.
Emil clears his throat.
The application was terrible, he says.
Gretchen laughs. Aw. That's too bad.
But, Emil says. It worked.

My father had created an application that nobody wanted. He didn't realize this, not entirely. The world had become so connected that there was no patience for an outdated model of correspondence. People had devices in their pockets that they could use to talk to anybody, anytime they wanted. Who needed a pen pal?

But he didn't know any better. He thought that it might be interesting to take away immediacy. I think that he thought if you had to wait for a very long time to receive a message from someone, perhaps when you responded, you would take more care with your words, and write things of greater value. So in a sense, I think he was a traditionalist. He hoped to bring the old ways into the new world, and to wring more pleasure out of this new world.

It didn't work, though. I searched and searched through the application, looking for other people who were using it, but there was nobody. I thought it was broken. I was paging through the directory, looking for other users, but everybody in the system was inactive.

Except for one person.

Their username was Icarus.

In this application, you could select a person to write to, and they would become your pen pal forever. You could never unchoose a person, and you could never choose another person. You became inextricably linked through my father's limited vision of how people would be connected.

There was nobody else to select, so I chose Icarus.

Did you write to Icarus? Gretchen asks.

I did, Emil says.

Did he write back?

He didn't.

That's too bad, Gretchen says.

But *she* did.

I had written a letter that was too personal for any pen pal. I think I had assumed that Icarus, whoever he was, would certainly not be actively participating in this lonely world my father had created. So while I began writing to Icarus, I found myself writing to my father instead. I wrote to him about all of the things that had transpired since the morning he died. I told him about my foster families, about school, about how I was just like him these days, how I couldn't sleep.

I sent the letter without thinking much about it, and then I skipped dinner with my foster family and just went to bed.

I forgot all about the letter, but I had rediscovered my father's old tablet computer, and I started to carry it with me everywhere. I did homework on it. I read books. I even slept with it under my pillow. It was all that was left of him, and it was precious to me.

Weeks must have passed before I got a letter from Icarus. By then, I'd completely forgotten writing the letter, and it all came back in a rush. I was embarrassed. What would this boy think of me? I'd spilled my guts to a stranger, but pretended that I was writing to my dad.

I was afraid to open the letter, but I did.

Dear Emil,

I was very pleased to receive your letter. I didn't think there were any other pen pals left in the world. Your letter arrived during a very trying week for me, so it was very nice to feel that there was something special for me. Someone chose to write me! Someone was interested in me!

As I read your letter I realized that my terrible week was not so terrible. I am so sorry about your father. (I think maybe you were writing to me by mistake. It didn't seem like you were that interested in who you were writing, just that writing what you had to write was very important. That's a big logical leap for me to make, so I'm sorry if I'm wrong!)

In any case, I hope we can still be pen pals anyway. I'd like very much to know that you are okay and feeling better, and that there are some happy things in your life despite all of the things that make you sad.

Some happy things we can talk about:

What is your middle name?
What color are your eyes?
Do you have a pet?
Have you ever seen a shooting star?
Do you like clowns? (They scare me.)

Please, please write back!

Your new friend,
Isona

Isona, Gretchen whispers. Pretty.

Her name was Isona Carus, Emil says. I. Carus. Icarus. I had just assumed.

Gretchen nods. Did you write her?

I did, for many, many years.

That's lovely. Did you meet?

We did more than that, Emil says.

Isona and I once counted how many letters we had written to each other. Altogether there were two thousand or so. When we started, I was thirteen years old, and she was sixteen. I lived in Butte, Montana, and she lived in Veria, Greece. I was a foster child, and she worked for her uncle in a cotton mill. Her world seemed far more real than my own. She seemed older, more experienced. I was just an immigrant child owned by the government, rented out to strange families who wanted to feel good about themselves.

But we wrote and wrote. She wrote to me about college, and I wrote about high school and my first after-school job, shelving books at a public library. She wrote about picking cotton seeds out of her clothing each night, and I told her about moving into a new foster home and sleeping in an unfamiliar bed.

We didn't meet until Isona was twenty-eight, and I was twenty-five. She was a college graduate, and had moved to Athens. She was a research assistant at a university, and I was starting medical school very late. She had encouraged me to do that. It was Isona who made me feel vital, like more than an orphan.

She came to America on a work project with a team of professors. They were going to be in Boston for three days, meeting with academics from all over the world. She told me she wished Boston was close to Montana.

I made it close.

I borrowed my friend's van -- I didn't have a car of my own -- and drove for forty hours, sleeping as little as I could. I spent most of my money paying highway tolls. When I got to Boston, I hadn't showered, I was exhausted, and I couldn't find Isona fast enough. I sat in the parking lot of the hotel she was staying in, and waited behind the wheel for her to walk out. She didn't answer my calls. I sent her text messages that she didn't answer.

In those days, it wasn't unusual to find out that someone you'd met online was not who they said they were. I'd been talking to Isona for twelve years -- half my life -- and I had never wondered if she was real. But sitting there in that van, I had the darkest thoughts. A beautiful teenage girl who lives in Greece? Who picks cotton and is studying archaeology?

Come on. She wasn't real. I'd fooled myself. She had sent photos over the years, but she'd probably stolen them from the Internet.

I fell asleep, a bundle of nerves. And I slept for eleven hours right there in the front seat of my friend's van.

And when I woke up --

Gretchen's head slides down Emil's chest.

-- she was there, he finishes.

He lifts Gretchen's head. Her eyes are closed, her mouth slightly open.

He kisses her forehead, then lowers her to the glass floor. He brushes the snow-white hair away from her eyes. He carefully extends her arms and legs, and tugs her gown to her knees. Below her, the dark side of the Earth has become light again, and the oceans seem a little brighter.

He presses a thumb to his wrist.

Nurse Allen answers. Yes, sir?

Send a gurney down, please, he says. Miss Gretchen has passed.

Yes, sir, Nurse Allen says. Oh, and Doctor? Nurse Lynne says that Miss Kyoh has arrived.

Tasneem, he says. I'll be there shortly.

Emil bends over Gretchen. You should have lived ten thousand years, he says.

With a heavy sigh, he gets to his feet and heads back into the corridors.

TASNEEM

Tasneem is waiting for him. She steps back to allow the orderlies to pass.

Be gentle with her, Emil says to the first orderly. She's precious.

Yes, sir, the orderly answers.

The two men disappear down the corridor, pushing an empty gurney ahead of them.

Doctor Widla, Tasneem says.

Oh, call me Emil, he says. It's good to see you.

And you, she says.

Walk with me, Tasneem.

They walk the length of the corridor together.

I saw your interview, he says, finally.

I think everybody did, Tasneem says. I've been contacted by a number of your patients, actually. They all want to know why I haven't died.

Why you haven't gone completely white, Emil says. Yes, I am not surprised. Do you have a theory? Have you had tests?

No tests, Tasneem says. But I do have a theory. That's why I came so quickly.

What is it?

Is there somewhere private we can go? she asks.

The lounge is, again, empty.

In here, Emil says.

He holds the door for Tasneem.

You can't tell anybody about this, she says.

I don't know if I can promise --

You must.

But if you have an idea about a cure --

I don't think I do, Tasneem says. I insist.

Alright, Tasneem. I promise.

Okay.

She removes something from her wrist, and he looks down to see a vintage wristband.

What's this? he asks.

Put it on, she says.

He wrinkles his forehead, but does as she instructs. The band does not fit him so well. It is tight around his wrist.

Now what? he asks.

Take a deep breath, Tasneem says. Exhale slowly.

Tasneem --

Do it, please, she says. You should be calm right now.

I'm calm, Tasneem.

Please, she says.

Emil inhales deeply, then breathes out in a patient rush.

Okay, he says. Now what.

I don't want you to be startled. Okay?

Tasneem, this is ridiculous. What are you talking --

Doctor Widla, says a strange voice. We haven't met. I'm David Dewbury.

Emil throws the wristband to the floor. What the *fuck*, he says. Who the fuck?

Tasneem picks up the band and puts it back on. I knew you'd be surprised, she says. I'm sorry.

What was that? Emil asks.

He is flustered, his eyes wide.

You remember David --

David fucking Dewbury, yes, yes, I remember. God fucking damn it, how could I not? Emil thrusts his fingers into his hair and begins to pace. The media would never let me forget. Why did you keep Soma from a genius? they asked me. As if I should have broken regulations for him! As if --

Doctor, Tasneem says. Please.

Emil stops speaking, but continues to pace. He stares at her.

David is not completely dead, she says.

Bullshit, Emil spits. Bullshit! I saw the body, Tasneem. I *saw* --

David's body is dead, Tasneem corrects. But David is not.

Emil stops pacing.

What the fucking hell are you saying? he says, finally.

I'm saying that the smartest man in the world is still with us, Tasneem says. And he has an idea.

REVOLUTION

The elderly were left behind.

Children were taken from their parents.

Entire towns and regions were excluded from the great migration.

Earth drowned. It burned. Cities were rebuilt, and destroyed again.

The fires were visible from space.

They never went out.

Generations of children were born who had never stepped on soil.

Man began to change.

In 2132, Station Tycho, named for the great astronomer, went online.

Three years later, Station Atlantis followed.

In the ensuing decades, five more stations -- Eden, Yuri, Virgo, Copernicus and Gan -- were deployed. Each housed more humans than the last. Fewer and fewer people were rescued from Earth below. The stations began to fill with new generations of space-born humans.

Earth's former leaders, presidents and kings and ministers, collaborated to govern mankind's fleet of lifeboats. For the first time in human history, a sort of peace was established. Men and women of all origins fell together, humans and survivors all, until mankind was no longer sortable. All were one. One were all.

In 2182, the great jewel of the fleet, Station Argus, was brought online.

Though few understood its implications, Argus and its social experiments represented great change.

The era of peace began to wane.

The uprisings would soon begin.

MICAH

ARGUS

What did you think of me? When you first saw me.
Well, I thought you were beautiful.
Really?
I thought, She has beautiful hair.
My hair. What about my eyes?
At first I couldn't see them. Not through your hair.
But then you did.
But then I did.
What did you think?
I thought, She has lovely eyes.
You did not.
I did. I really did.
Do you still think so?
I do. I always will.
Always is a very long time. It's the longest time.
It could never be long enough for me.
You're sweet. Do you think that will ever happen?
Do I think what will happen? Us? Always?
Yes. Us, for always.

It could. I think it could happen.

Don't you think you'd get tired of me? Everyone gets bored with everyone else.

I would be grateful for every moment, forever.

Grateful to who?

I don't know. To the universe.

That's easy to say now.

It's easy to say things that are true.

But you think you mean it.

I know I mean it.

Do you think that in one hundred years we'll remember this?

This conversation?

This. The conversation. You, there. Me, here. Us, together.

I think we'll still be having this conversation.

I'm going to pretend you meant that in a nice way.

I did. I meant it in the most wonderful way.

The young man stares quietly through the window. He stands with his hands in his pockets. His shoulders are tired and slump a little. The satchel over his left shoulder scoots down a little. Without thinking about it, he pushes the strap back up. His knees are bent, as if he's being pressed down by some unseen thumb.

He sighs.

In the glass he can see the reflection of people milling around him. Most of them are doing just what he's doing:

staring out into the dark.

Beside him, an old man in a sweater stands next to a little girl. He holds the girl's hand. The girl holds a rich orange gerbera daisy in her other hand. The vibrant color reminds the young man of autumn on the island.

There you are.

Good morning.

I don't know why I thought you would be anywhere else. It's so pretty here.

I like to watch the fog peel away from the water in the morning.

You're even literary when you talk. I like that.

Is that for me?

I made two cups. They're both for me.

Funny girl.

Silly man. I'm glad you brought me here. It's gorgeous. The leaves are starting to fall.

My grandparents used to bring me here when I was small. It was always cooler here than on the mainland. I used to run around on the lawn and kick through the leaves. There was almost always a steep wind off the water, so the leaves would sort of tornado around me, like they were trying to get away.

Did they live here?

My grandparents?

Yes.

No. They lived in northern California, just where the rolling hills turned to scrub. But Grandpa had a friend -- from the war, I think -- who owned this place, and let them use it once a year. Almost always in the fall.

How many times did you come?

Oh, I don't remember. The first time they brought me here, I think I was seven. Maybe eight. The last time was the year I was a junior in high school. The year Grandma died.

Do you miss her?

I do. I miss them both.

You brought me here. That's pretty special.

I tried to think of the most wonderful place.

There's no place more wonderful?

Not on Earth.

Ah, so there are possibilities.

Even if there are, I wouldn't care. You can't argue with this place.

It does have a special pull.

That's exactly what it has.

Like a gravitational force.

Sure. I guess.

The old man elbows him.

At first the younger man ignores this. There are enough people around the windows that he has been jostled several times already.

But then the old man elbows him again, and the younger man turns.

The old man smiles broadly, all teeth. He raises the little girl's hand and nods at it, then leans in and says, Do you think she appreciates this? Do you think she can even understand how precious this moment is?

The younger man rocks forward on his toes and looks at the girl more closely. She stares through the glass with a blank expression. Her hands are content to be still. Her fingers don't so much as twirl the stem of the daisy that rests against her collarbone. She's precious herself, small and delicate in a knee-length polka-dotted dress and dark shoes with tiny buckles. Her strawberry-blonde hair frames her freckled face in ringlets.

She's seven, the old man says.

When I was seven, I'm not sure I would have, the younger man says.

The old man frowns at this, then reconsiders, and smiles once more. But you're not seven now. You and I, I think we recognize this moment for what it is. You're a young buck, but I think you know.

I'm old enough, the younger man says.

So am I, the old man agrees. I've waited a very long time to see this. Now that it's here, I'm too interested in what other people think I think about it to feel the way I think I feel about it.

What other people?

The old man waves dismissively at the crowd that mills around them. Eh, he grunts. They're just people. Strangers, the whole lot of them. I take your point. I shouldn't let it bother me.

The younger man turns back to the window. Outside it is a

starless night. The Earth is somewhere below, the moon somewhere behind. One of them casts a pale pool of light on the approaching wall, but he cannot tell which. Mae would have known.

Looming large in the window is the enormous crystalline flower of the space station, its petals cast open to reveal an interior of glittering spires and complex geometric structures. These are visible only for a moment, and then the shuttle passes below the station's horizon line. The beautiful surface modules disappear, and all the younger man can see are shuttle bays, dozens of them marked with reflective panels and pulsing caution lights.

This is so exciting, the old man says. I've waited so long for this moment.

The younger man grunts.

The old man looks at him with surprise. Not you?

The younger man says, Not particularly. No.

The old man opens his mouth to reply, but is interrupted before he can begin. The little girl tugs at his hand.

Grandpa, she says. I'm sleepy.

Okay, sweetheart, the old man says.

He crouches next to her and opens his arms. Up?

She nods, and steps into his embrace, resting her head on his shoulder. The old man closes his arms around her, tucks her knees in, and struggles to stand up.

The younger man offers a hand.

The old man grips it fiercely and pulls. The younger man did not expect such force, and locks his elbow and draws the old man to his feet.

Thank you, the old man says.

The girl stares obliquely into the distance as the old man gently sways.

The younger man returns his gaze to the window. The slow acceleration towards the docking bays has halted. Another much smaller shuttle drifts into view, adjusting tiny attitude jets to propel it gently into a lower bay. He watches it settle into place and sink on its broad duck feet.

The old man says, I didn't mean to offend you before.

The younger man turns. No offense. Really.

How impolite of me, the old man says. I should remember that not everybody cares what I think.

Not at all, says the younger man. Truly.

The old man regards him carefully, then adjusts his granddaughter in his arms and extends one hand. I'm Bernard, he says.

Micah, says the younger man.

Micah, the old man repeats.

Bernard nods in Micah's direction as the shuttle empties. Micah waits at the window a little longer, until the stream of passengers spills across the deck below like a box of brightly-colored candies. He is not entirely sure what he had expected from the journey, but so far it reminds him of little so much as a cattle car.

When he steps onto the landing platform, he pauses to collect himself. His fellow passengers, most of them, have swarmed to the processing checkpoints, where attendees in glass cubicles study and stamp paperwork and wave people on to their new homes. But a few mill about, perhaps waiting for the dishearteningly long processing lines to dwindle. Micah looks for a familiar face and sees none, though there is a middle-aged man standing next to a baggage trolley, alone.

Micah adjusts his satchel and starts to walk towards the stranger. He doesn't really want to talk to the man, but he also feels uncomfortable here, disconnected from other people among a crowd of partners and posses.

An electronic squeal bursts from the shuttle, and the passengers jump and stare up at the shuttle in alarm.

A voice says, NO DALLYING, PLEASE.

Micah cringes. It's louder than any voice he's ever heard, and he remembers what rock concerts were like, once. He casts about, looking for the owner of the voice, and spies him, a tiny, rotund man in an administrator's uniform and white cap.

The little man speaks into his hand again. PLEASE CONTINUE TO THE ARRIVALS PROCESSING CHECKPOINT IMMEDIATELY.

As his fellow passengers grumble and fall into line, Micah catches the administrator's eye.

He offers a small wave and a smile.

The administrator cocks his head, then, quite slowly, raises one small, gloved hand.

Micah stands at the end of the line, alone. Ahead of him, the trail of passengers winds forward like a knot of licorice, uneven and clumped in places. He reaches into his pocket and plucks out a small gray card. It glimmers slightly. Its corners are rounded beads of fine glass. The card is blank save for a tiny engraved rectangle on the back.

He doesn't want it.

The line moves at a glacial pace. Micah takes advantage of this to look around. There's nothing particularly remarkable about this, his first close look at the interior of a space station. The landing deck is vast, and his shuttle is not the only one that has landed here to deposit its human payload. Micah squints and counts three more shuttles. The space between each is easily a quarter mile. He thinks about how many shuttle bays he saw during the approach -- there were probably fifty or more.

He approximates the math. If each shuttle bay is a mile wide and half as deep, and there are fifty bays...

He blinks. The station is even larger than he had imagined.

Ahead, there is a disturbance in the line. He can hear scuffling and raised voices. He takes a step to his left to get a better view, and sees an administrator in a red uniform and white gloves. The administrator is waving his hands at the people in line, several of whom look like they might revolt.

I understand your frustration, the administrator is saying.

It's not easy to hear, but Micah watches anyway. The crowd pushes against him. A woman leans in close and shouts something at the administrator, who takes a step back and speaks into his wrist. Micah sees movement at the periphery of his vision and turns to see several more people in uniforms rushing to the administrator's aid.

Within moments, the uniformed newcomers have quelled the crowd. The administrator speaks to one man in particular, and that man steps out of line.

The man is immaculately and expensively dressed. His hair is perfectly coiffed, and he stands straight and tall and confident.

The man is holding a small gray card.

Micah puts his own card back into his pocket.

The administrator takes the man's bag from him and escorts him away from the line. Micah watches as they approach a series of freestanding clear tubes. The administrator stops in front of one of the tubes. The tube stretches upward to the ceiling, which itself seems to be many miles away, its detail hazy and obscured by distance. The bottom of the tube rotates, and Micah can see that there is an outer and an inner layer. These rotate in opposite directions until they align, revealing an opening wide enough for the administrator and his guest to step through.

The tube's layers rotate again, sealing the two men inside. A moment later, the men are levitated upward.

Micah and his fellow passengers watch the two men float higher within the tube. Then they disappear through the ceiling, two small packages whisked away to some unknown destination.

Micah fingers the card inside of his pocket dubiously.

Lucky bastard, someone says.

He's not the only one, says another.

She's correct. Administrators are scuttling up and down the passenger lines like beetles. Here and there they pry a passenger out of line. Each of these selected passengers are well-dressed.

Each bears a small gray card.

Would you ever want to live someplace else?

I don't know. I like it here.

I know. And it's beautiful. But what about someplace equally beautiful?

You aren't happy here?

I am. Of course I am. Micah -- I am.

Is there someplace you want to go? Morocco or someplace?

Well...

There is. And it's better than this? Better than the ocean and the orange trees and the rain?

Micah, this place is lovely. I'm so happy you brought me here.

But you want to leave.

I don't know why we can't just have a conversation.

Alright. Fine. Let's talk about it.

Not like this. It's not even important. It's not even real. Forget about it.

I can't forget about it. Clearly this is important to you.

Micah --

Well, where is it? France? Australia?

Micah.

Belgium? Maybe Portugal is a nicer place than this.

You're being cruel.

I'm not. Tell me where.

It's none of those places. It's not important.

Italy?

Micah.

Is it Italy?

No, it's not Italy.

Alright. Which direction from Italy?

Micah. Jesus.

Which direction?

Up.

What? Up?

Up.

Okay. Alaska. Greenland.

Up.

The Arctic Circle. That's got to be it. You want to live on an icebreaker ship, saving polar bears. That's obviously better than here.

Up.

The North Pole.

More up.

There's no more up you can go!

You're not listening to me. You never listen when you get like this.

Look, the North Pole is the top. There's no more up.

You weren't listening.

All I do is listen to you!

I didn't say north, asshole. I said up.

Bernard and his granddaughter are somewhere in the middle of the line. The girl is still on his shoulder, but sleeping now.

Micah falls out of the line and quickly walks to where the old man is standing.

Hey, someone says.

Micah turns and, walking backward, says, No, no, I'm not jumping the line. It's okay.

He reaches Bernard and puts his hand on the old man's shoulder. Bernard, he says.

Bernard turns. He is sweating profusely.

Micah, the old man says.

Are you okay?

Bernard nods at the girl. She is not a little bird any more. But she is tired, and so for now, I will hold her as long as I can.

It's a long line, though, Micah says.

You are an astute observer, Bernard replies, not without some sarcasm.

I brought you something, Bernard. Here.

Bernard's eyebrows raise. Oh?

Here, Micah repeats.

Bernard looks down and sees Micah's hand holding a gray card. The old man's eyes widen. What are you doing, Micah? he asks. Do you know what that is?

Sort of, Micah says.

You don't have to be here, man. Go!

Bernard turns, looking about for an administrator.

Micah grabs his shoulder. No, he says. I want you to take it.

Bernard jostles the woman ahead of him in line. She whirls about.

I'm sorry, Bernard says. But the woman's irritation is defused by the card she sees in Micah's hand.

Dear god, she says. You have a card? You have a card!

No, Micah says. No, it's --

Who has a card? someone else says.

This man here has a card, the woman says.

Micah turns back to Bernard. I want you to have this, he says. Please.

He tries to push the card into Bernard's hand, but the old man snatches his hand away. What are you doing? Micah!

Take it, Micah repeats.

It is too much, Bernard protests. It is too valuable. I can't.

Give it to me, the woman interrupts, reaching for the card.

Micah turns away from her. It's not for you, he says.

If you're giving it away, I want it, someone else says.

Micah presses the card into Bernard's hand again. Please. It would help you.

The line begins to come apart around the two men. Strangers surge into the gaps, pushing.

I'll take it! someone shouts.

Give it to me!

I must have it! It would change my baby's life!

Please!

Me!

Give it!

Micah takes advantage of the commotion to close Bernard's fingers around the card. The old man looks confused to find the card in his hand, and Micah tries to melt away in the mob of passengers.

What's happening here? a deep voice booms.

Instantly the crowd begins to dissolve, and Micah sees one of the red-suited administrators stalking towards him. He's carrying a baton in one hand.

Nothing, someone says.

Everything's fine!

I didn't do it!

It's not mine!

The administrator spies the card in Bernard's hand. His gaze shifts to Bernard's worried face, then back to the card.

Sir, the administrator says to Bernard.

It's not his card, someone snitches.

The administrator turns toward the passengers behind Bernard, then looks back at Bernard. Is this true? Is this your card?

Bernard is petrified. His granddaughter starts awake, her face flushed.

Grandpa? she says, her voice fuzzy with sleep.

Sir? Is that card yours?

Bernard holds up the card, unable to find his voice.

It's mine, Micah says, stepping forward.

Bernard's entire body relaxes, and the card falls to the floor.

The administrator puts the toe of his boot on the card. He studies Micah's face carefully, then his attire.

This card belongs to you? he asks Micah.

Micah nods. It does.

This man did not steal it from you? The administrator indicates Bernard with his baton.

Bernard tenses at the sight of the stick pointed in his direction.

Micah reaches out and tips the baton toward the floor. The administrator steps back quickly.

Absolutely he didn't steal it, Micah says. I wanted to give it to him.

The administrator looks suspicious. You wanted to give him your Onyx card.

Bernard finds his voice. I didn't try to take it!

Onyx cards are not transferable, the administrator says sternly.

I didn't want it! Bernard cries.

I didn't know that, Micah says.

I find that difficult to believe, the administrator says. Every Onyx cardholder knows that the card is not transferable.

I didn't, Micah says. I inherited it from my wife.

From your wife, the administrator echoes.

She's gone, Micah says. I wanted to give the card away.

Bernard looks at Micah. His expression changes. All of his alarm and tension vanishes, and in its place is a look of such pure compassion that Micah has to turn away. He knows that look. He's seen it before, on other faces. On the faces of people who have lost people. On the faces of people who still feel the prick of loss every morning when they turn over in bed.

It doesn't really work that way, sir, the administrator says.

I didn't know that.

It's alright, the administrator says. Then he turns his mouth into his wrist and says something that Micah doesn't quite hear.

Micah glances at Bernard, who is still looking at him with those terribly sad eyes.

It's okay, Micah mouths at him.

Bernard shakes his head sadly and mouths something back that looks like, So young.

Then an escort in a soft gray uniform arrives, and the administrator says to Micah, Please, allow Mr. Hedderly to take your bag.

The escort smiles at Micah. His teeth are impossibly white. Every last one of them is perfectly placed and perfectly visible. May I, sir?

Micah sighs and looks at Bernard, and then at the administrator. Couldn't I just stay in line?

Behind him, a woman says, He did *not* just say that.

I'm afraid not, sir, the administrator says. May I?

He holds his hand out for the card.

Micah gives it to him.

Your thumb, sir.

The administrator turns the card over to reveal the rectangle printed there.

Micah sighs again, then presses his thumb down on the rectangle. The card lights up, and Mae's face appears on its surface. Her name, identification code, and physical attributes are drawn in beside it.

Mae Isabella Atherton-Sparrow
0522FG010-EPG
H 5'3"   W 112

Micah stares at the photograph of Mae. He remembers the day that they visited the Settlement Transition Bureau. They had fought that day. He hadn't wanted to go, which was usually enough to deter Mae. That day had been different. She had gone anyway, without telling him, and it wasn't until weeks later that he found the Onyx card in her bag while he was looking for the chocolates she often kept hidden there. He had been angry.

The photograph was perhaps the most beautiful picture of Mae he had ever seen. It was low-quality, with artifacts that interrupted the image. Like most global agencies, the STB didn't spend much on equipment. It didn't matter how bad the photograph itself was. The image of Mae that shone through was beautiful because of her expression.

It was the purest expression of happiness and hope. Her eyes were alive, brighter and larger than life. Her smile stretched wider than he had imagined possible, shoving her round cheeks high. Her skin was flushed, as if she couldn't believe what was happening, couldn't contain her excitement.

He had never seen her so happy before.

You don't mean --
   Yes. Up.
   Up.
   Yes.

I can't.

You have to admit it would be beautiful.

But I... I. Up?

Up, Micah. Up there. It would be beautiful, too. Not like this, but beautiful in other ways. Beautiful because it would mean something... more.

It's a million miles away.

Well, no. It's not.

Fine, okay. Not a million, but it might as well be. Jesus, Mae.

I didn't know you felt strongly about it.

I feel strongly about Earth! Under my feet! I like standing here. Do you know who built this pier? No? Well, I do. His name was Marcus Perrine, and he was twenty-eight when he built it with his bare hands as a gift for his bride. It's been here for nearly eighty years. There's history here. I like history.

There's history there, too. More history, even.

Don't be ridiculous. It's not the same.

You really wouldn't? For me?

I'm not a spaceman, Mae.

You wouldn't even think about it?

I'm from Earth. What's up there that isn't here? Don't scientists spend their careers looking for places just like Earth? Why do you think that is? It's because its Earths that matter. They're rare and precious and beautiful and amazing. And I like living here. It smells nice. It makes my heart happy.

Not even for me?

Mae.

Micah.

You're asking so much.

It would be the grandest adventure. It would be thrilling every day.

No, it wouldn't. It would be terribly boring.

I've dreamed of going there since they built the first one. Galileo. I was eight.

You've dreamed of moving to space since you were eight years old.

Yes! Yes, Micah. I wanted to watch the sun rise.

What do you think we just watched?

Not here, Micah. To watch the sun rise over the entire planet. I want to float! I want to float like a feather. I want to --

You want to live in a dark cold scary vacuum that will kill you.

Yes. I do, I do! Because we tamed it, Micah. Look what we did! Look up, you can even see them up there now.

I don't want to look up.

Now you're just being petulant.

Living in orbit would make me miserable.

How do you --

Some things you just know. You just do.

You really wouldn't even consider it?

What about our families, Mae? What about Christmases and Thanksgivings and birthdays?

Maybe they'll all come with us. Who knows! Don't you think being a part of something greater than yourself is worth missing a few family holidays?

Not a few, Mae. All of them. Or didn't you know that you can't come back?

I knew it.

So, really, you're okay with leaving our families forever. Is that what they mean to you?

You're missing the point, Micah.

Oh, am I.

I've always wondered what an impasse feels like.

Don't be dramatic.

Well, what would you call it?

So we're doomed, is that it? Because I don't want to be a spaceman with you?

Don't make light.

Look. Mae. I love you. You know I do.

I need a few minutes.

You know I'd do anything for you.

Micah, give me a minute. Okay?

I should go inside?

Forget it. I will.

Wait. Mae, wait.

The image of Mae and her details disappear from the card. A simple red line of text appears in its place.

Deceased January 7 2178

The administrator glances up at Micah, then back down at the card. He touches it with two fingers, and the red text disappears. A single small dot dances on the card. The administrator says, Inheritor.

Micah blinks, only now realizing that his eyes are damp.

The blinking dot vanishes, and a new profile appears. Where the photo should be, there is a simple empty box.

Micah Roderick Sparrow

0627J007-1211-E

H 5'11" W 192

You can remove your thumb now, the administrator says. Stand up straight, Mr. Sparrow.

The administrator holds the card at Micah's eye level. The surface of the card reflects Micah's face back at him. He is startled to see that he has two long tear-streaks on his skin, and he quickly wipes them away with the heels of his palms.

Big smile, the administrator says. One. Two. Three. Snap!

The image on the card freezes.

The administrator turns the card over and looks at the image, then up at Micah. Maybe one more try? he says.

Micah shakes his head.

The image is the exact opposite of Mae's. Micah's expression is one of a lost soul.

Unlike Mae's beautiful smile, Micah has seen this expression on his face every day for two years.

Mr. Sparrow, says the escort in the gray suit. Shall we?

Micah looks at Bernard. I'm sorry, he says.

Bernard nods. Me, too.

I meant --

I know what you meant. Be well, Micah.

The escort takes the Onyx card from the administrator and returns it to Micah.

Micah absently tucks it into his pocket.

Mr. Sparrow, the administrator says, extending his hand. Welcome to Argus Station.

ONYX

What are you doing?
Reading. You're in my light.
Maybe we should talk about this.
I don't want to.
It's important that we work these things out. Otherwise what are we?
I don't want to talk about it, Micah.
Mae.
Leave me alone.
What are you reading?
Leave me alone, please.
We'll talk about it later.
Whatever.

Micah stares at his reflection in the mirror. He is older than he remembers. He has crows' feet on either side of his tired brown eyes. When he concentrates, it looks like someone has pulled a rake across his forehead. There are fault lines, deep ones, framing his mouth. The effect is that his face looks as if it has been assembled from several pieces. He forces an inauthentic smile and watches the lines deepen and shift.

He sighs, and bends over the sink and splashes water on his face.

The sun has broken over the Earth since he last looked outside. The view from his apartment makes him ill. He pads barefoot across the chamber to a window that spans the entire exterior wall, from the floor of his apartment to the high ceiling. The glass is deeply tinted, but the orange glow that suffuses the city below is powerful all the same.

He touches the glass with all five fingers, then rotates his hand slightly to his right. A faint contrail appears beneath his fingers. Above it is a readout: 90/100. As he turns his hand, the number climbs, and the window darkens measurably. He turns his hand to the left. The number falls to 74/100, and Micah has to close his eyes against the fierce brightness that the weaker shade has revealed.

He rotates his hand to the right blindly until his eyelids are no longer shot through with angry red darts. For a while after he opens them again, his vision is imprinted with slashes of red that turn white and disappear after a few seconds.

He squeezes his eyes shut tightly, then flexes his fingers as wide as they will go. He holds this stretching position until his hands tremble, then exhales slowly, relaxing the muscles in his hands just as slowly. When he has relaxed completely, his hands are like soggy hunks of bread, invisible in the tactile spectrum of nerves that make up his identity.

The apartment would please anybody. Three thousand square feet, richly furnished, with a floor that absorbs his weight and is so soft that he could sleep on it if he chose. The bed is positioned in such a way that he will wake to a view of Argus City each morning, with its spires and towering spacescrapers and humming air traffic. The walls are designed in moveable sets, so that Micah can adjust the apartment's layout to suit his needs.

He has no interest in the floor plan.

Micah rotates his hand on the window until it becomes opaque. The window vanishes, its interior surface now the same color as the apartment's walls.

If desired, I can apply some digital art to these walls, a voice says.

I don't desire, Micah says.

He crosses the room to the bed.

Shall I adjust the climate to complement your resting body temperature?

Do whatever you want, Micah says.

He stretches out in the bed, grips one of the spare pillows as if it is another warm body, and tries to sleep.

The escort in the gray suit had had plenty to say about Micah's new environment. After their stomach-turning ride through the giant transport tubes, during which Micah had watched a dozen decks full of new arrivals zoom by, the escort had given Micah a brief tour.

Don't you have other visitors to meet? Micah had asked, annoyed.

Oh, no, the escort replied. Each Onyx resident has a dedicated escort for their first week. After that week, the escorts are less vital, and more of a convenience. There are usually four of us for each petal floor.

How many residents are on each floor?

Approximately two hundred, the escort answered.

And how many floors?

Each petal has five hundred floors. There are ten petals altogether, he added.

Micah was surprised. The station seems like it could support more than just a million people, he said. That's only a tenth of the population of most of the big cities in America.

The escort nodded. This way, he said.

Micah followed the escort across a grand lobby. At the nearest end, the lobby looked into the heart of Argus City. He stopped and stared for a moment, his eyes following one canyon between the tall buildings as far as he could, until the city faded into a blue haze and lost all definition.

How far across is the city? he asked.

Two hundred forty miles, sir.

Two hundred forty miles of city for just one million people? That seems... wasteful.

The escort shook his head. Oh, no, sir. One million is the number of Onyx residents, but Onyx-class residents are just a small percentage of Argus's total occupancy.

I don't understand, Micah said.

On the arrival deck, the escort said. All of the other new arrivals? Your fellow passengers on the shuttle?

Micah remembered.

Well, sir, they comprise the Machine-class residents.

Machine-class?

Machine-class, the escort repeated. As in, they are the machine that keeps Station Argus going.

I don't understand, Micah said again.

Don't worry, the escort said, striking off toward another series of lift tubes. Everything will be explained.

Where were you this afternoon?

Out.

Mae, can we stop being so hostile?

I'm not being hostile. That's where I was. Out.

This is so exhausting.

I don't know what's so exhausting about it.

This.

This what?

This whole argument. It's... it's seeping into who we are.

I don't know what you mean.

Yes, you do. Look, I know you want to go to space. Okay? I know. I'm sorry that I don't.

It's not that simple. And I don't want to talk about it.

We have to talk about it. We have to get past this.

No, Micah. No, we don't. We can't.

Can't?

You really don't understand this, do you.

Understand what? We both have things that we wish we could do that we won't ever get to do.

Well, thanks for deciding for me.

Come on, Mae.

Don't patronize me.

It feels like this isn't going to get better.

You just want me to put this back in the box I took it out of. I know what you want, Micah. You want what you always get. You want your way.

That's not what I want.

It is! And it's what you always get, too. It's the idea of my having dreams that you like. You think it makes me adorable and interesting. But it's the reality of my having dreams that you hate, because it might upend your happy routine.

Jesus. Mae, is that what you think?

I don't have to think it, Micah. It's obvious.

I don't hate the idea of you having dreams.

You missed the point. That's not what I said. You hate the reality *of my having dreams.*

I don't, either.

Then I want to go to space. And I want you to come with me, Micah. As my husband, the man who I want to build a future with. Come with me! We'll raise our family there, and our children will grow up at the changing, exciting edge of history. They'll tell their children one day, and their grandchildren, that they were raised in space, one of the first couple of generations to do it. They'll be like the pioneers who set out for California, or the first immigrants to America. Let's go, Micah. Let's go to space and look down at the Earth and up at the stars. They'll be closer than ever, almost close enough to touch. Let's be there when we get tired of living in orbit, and we decide it's time to go wherever is next. We'll be old then, but we can say, Wow, look at humanity go! Look at how far we've --

Mae, I don't want to live in space. I want to live right here, in this house on this shore with this view and this rain and this creaky old pier and these trees. I want our kids to plant their own trees in this yard and watch them grow to a hundred feet tall. I want them to carve little notches in the door frames each year to see how much they've grown. I want to fill this house with a lifetime of our things so that one day there's this pleasant clutter that we'll always find some memory buried in. I want a happy and long life right here, Mae. And I want you with me.

I know all of that, Micah. And don't worry. You'll win. You'll get to have all of that.

Mae, come on --

No. No, that's what you want. I know. You want me to sulk for a couple of days, then get over it, and we'll get old and wrinkly and pretend that there was never a time when we fought about this. You might actually forget about it for real. In fact, I know you will. That's what you do. You've got one big-ass rug in your brain, Micah, and you're really good at sweeping shit under it that you never want to see again.

Mae, please --

No! No, that's what's going to happen. You'll be this oblivious, cheerful old man, and all of our grandchildren will love you because you're so happy, because you're living the perfect life you've always dreamed of, and every day is just a vacation for you. And they'll have less of a connection with me, because they'll know, somehow, somewhere deep inside, that something isn't quite right about

Grandma. They won't know what it is, but they'll be able to tell, because when a person has a dream that they've dreamed of their whole life, and they don't get a single chance to accomplish it in the single life that belongs to them, they just sort of wither inside, Micah, they dry up and rot on the inside, and the nice thing is that nobody can see it on the outside, not really well, so everybody else can pretend that everything is okay. But not me, Micah. I'll get the great pleasure of dying a little inside every single day that you get to have the life you want, and I have to put my own dreams in a fucking box and fucking burn it.

You're on the eighty-fifth floor, the escort had said. I hope you're not afraid of heights. And if you are, just imagine two things. First, remember that there are four hundred fifteen floors that are even higher than yours.

And second? Micah asked.

Oh, just that you're already thirty thousand miles above the place where you were born, the escort said cheerfully.

That's reassuring, Micah said. Is it really thirty thousand miles?

Thirty-two thousand miles, six hundred feet. Or something like that.

Huh, Micah said. Hey, before -- before you said that everything would be explained. You know that my Onyx card isn't actually mine, right?

You inherited it, the escort said. Right. Don't worry about

that. We have quite a few inheritors. It's not unusual to inherit an Onyx card without having taken the classes.

There are classes?

Oh, yes. Every Onyx-class candidate takes a twelve-week course on Earth after they're identified.

What sort of classes? Micah had asked.

Oh, everything from what to expect from an artificial-grav environment to how to interact effectively with an A.I. to a history series about the stations, the escort said. Pretty basic orientation stuff, really.

So what do, um, inheritors do to learn this stuff?

I'll introduce you to your A.I., the escort said. Let's zip up to your floor, then.

My A.I.? Micah had asked.

Sure. It'll be great, don't worry.

Do I have to have an A.I.? What if I just want to be alone?

Oh, that's the best part, the escort said. You just tell the A.I. to go away. Just say, Bob, I'd like to be alone. And there you go.

Bob?

Well, you can name yours whatever you want. I'm sure somebody chose Bob for theirs.

But not you?

Oh, I don't have an A.I., Mr. Sparrow.

You don't? Micah asked. Why not? That seems unfair.

I'm Machine-class, sir, the escort said.

Machine-class.

It's grand, sir, the escort said cheerfully. Your A.I. will teach you all about it. I'm sure you'll enjoy it.

Machine-class, Micah repeated.

Yes, sir. Let's take the lift now, shall we?

And up they went.

I don't think you should go.

It's not up to you.

Maybe. I guess. But I wish you wouldn't.

This is kind of serious, Micah. It's a good opportunity for me at work. If I do well, it might change the way they perceive me. Who knows, it could turn into a promotion, even.

I don't like you going away when we're in the middle of a fight.

I don't like fighting with you, Micah.

I don't like fighting with you, either. We should just call a cease-fire. Truce.

That only works when it's not an important fight. It won't work for this.

What if you don't come back?

Is that what you're afraid of?

I'm afraid you won't come back.

I'll come back. Even if it's just to get my stuff.

That's not funny.

I know.

Are you serious?

I think a little break will put things in perspective, Micah. But it's not going to change my point.

Then why take a break? We'll be in the same place then that we are now.

Because I'm tired of sleeping badly because we're both all worked-up over this. It'll be good for us. You need the break, too.

I don't. I don't want it.

Micah, it's just two weeks. I'm going to be working. You'll be working. We'll hardly notice it.

I'll notice it.

Micah.

I will. I'll come home to this place, empty. You'll go home to a fancy hotel, probably nice dinners with your boss, who knows what.

Don't imply anything. That's not going to help.

I'm sorry. I can't help it. I'm a wreck thinking about you leaving.

You'll have this place to yourself again. You love it here. It'll be good for you.

I don't want it to myself.

Micah. Make the most of the two weeks. Think about something else. Work on a project.

I could build the crib. The one we talked about.

Don't do that.

What? Why not?

Micah, don't do that. You know what you're doing. Don't do that. Build a bookcase or something.

Shit. You aren't coming back, are you. You're really not coming back, and you already know it. You're just dragging this out. Well, if that's what you're going to do, then do it. Rip it off, Mae. Do it.

Micah, it's a work trip. I'm coming back.

You don't want me to build the crib.

You're just being awful to yourself if you build it, Micah. We aren't ready for kids and won't be any time soon. We have real things to figure out here.

I can't believe that moving to space is the thing we have to figure out. I can't believe moving to space is the thing that might ruin us.

Well, that's a problem. You even treat the idea of this problem like a joke.

Oh, I didn't mean it like that, Mae. I --

I think you did. Look, I'm going to pack. We can talk a bit more tonight, and in the morning I have to fly out. My flight is at six, so I'll be gone early.

Where's the trip to?

Tokyo.

Where are you staying?

I don't know. I have the itinerary somewhere. You can have a copy, okay? But Micah, I want to treat this like a time-out. I don't want to talk to you every night. I don't want to hear about your day. I want time to think about our future without you putting your foot in your mouth.

I can't even call?

Look. I love you. I have always loved you, and I always will, no matter what. But Micah, you think that my biggest, most life-long dream is a farce, and you're standing in the way of me ever even having a chance to accomplish it. So yes, we have things to figure out, and no, I don't want to talk to you for a little while.

I don't think it's a farce.

Micah --

Say whatever you want, Mae. I don't think it's a farce. It just... scares me.

Alright, we're done.

Hey --

No. Every time we fight, if there's a real problem we can't work out, you play-act this emotional psychobabble moment of discovery, like you've just come to terms with something about yourself. But it's a

goddamn trick, Micah. I'm supposed to see how vulnerable you are,
and come running to you and comfort you. But it's just a diversion. I
don't even think you know you're doing it. But I'm going upstairs to
pack, and we can talk about this in two weeks when I come home and
we've both had time to really think about what we want to do next.

I don't do that. Mae? I don't do that. Mae, come on.

Micah starts awake to a blinding light. He turns over in bed,
throws his arm over his eyes.

The window is transparent again.

He says, What the hell?

The A.I. speaks up. You were in your optimum sleep state
for waking, Micah. Gradual light is a positive way to emerge
from a restful state.

Gradual, hell. Close the window.

As you wish, Micah.

The window becomes opaque again.

Hours later Micah awakes on his own. The apartment is
completely dark. He rolls over and swings his feet over the
edge of the bed.

You are awake, the A.I. says. May I provide anything for

you?

Don't talk to me when I wake up, Micah says. You can start with that.

Very well.

Micah pads into the kitchen, barefoot. The floor is almost spongy beneath his feet. As much as he misses the water-logged planks of the pier back home, he must admit that this is nice.

He touches the door of the pantry. It hisses open like an airlock. Micah frowns. He misses the old tacky sound of his refrigerator opening. Everything in the apartment sounds like a television show's idea of the future. He looks around for a toaster but doesn't see one. If there was one, it would probably sound like a ray gun.

The pantry is empty. Micah goes around the kitchen, opening panels one by one. There's nothing inside. The cooling closet is empty as well.

A.I., he says, finally.

Yes, Micah.

I think I need to buy food. I don't know how to do that.

Micah, if you'll join me in the dining space, I'll be pleased to explain how to acquire food, the A.I. says.

Your speech is weird, Micah says as he walks into the dining room.

Define weird, the A.I. replies.

The voice seems to emerge from the air. There are no visible speakers in the apartment, and the A.I. has no visible avatar or physical body of any kind. It's simply... there.

Weird, Micah repeats. You know, oddly formal but sometimes not formal at all. It's like a blend of two completely different cultures.

Let's select a voice pattern that you'll identify with, the A.I. suggests. Please sit. Do you prefer a male voice, a female voice, or an androgynous voice?

Micah thinks about this. Female, he says, finally.

He hears three faint tones.

How's this? the A.I. says.

The almost sterile travel-guide voice of the A.I. has been replaced with that of a female.

Say something else, Micah says. Tell me about the weather.

Unfortunately, there is no natural weather in space, the A.I. says. I can tell you about the simulated weather events and the schedule by which they occur.

No, that's okay, Micah says. That's enough. How much can you modify the female voice?

You have several variables to select from, the A.I. says. You may modify the masculinity or femininity of my voice. You may select regional influences. You may adjust the formality or informality of my speech. You may even provide me with an input sample that I may mimic as closely as possible.

Micah considers this. Your voice is a little flat. Maybe it could sound a little, I don't know, warmer? More friendly.

Like this? the A.I. asks.

Say something else.

The simulated air flow adopts a weaving pattern through the city, carrying a pleasant breeze down each street, and modulating the --

That's enough, Micah says. That's better. Friendly-sounding but not too intimate.

If you would like to adjust for intimacy at a later time, you may modify my voice settings at your leisure, the A.I. says.

What do you mean by intimacy? Micah says.

There are multiple definitions of the word, the A.I. explains. You may adjust my properties for most of them. If you prefer me to address you in more personal ways, or assume a deeper history than we actually possess, then I can adjust my words to approximate that sort of intimacy. However, some users on the station prefer their A.I. to address them with content which is more intimate.

You mean they like their A.I.s to talk dirty to them, Micah says.

If by dirty you mean speech which has sexual or provocative content, then you are correct.

Isn't that a little -- I don't know -- low-tech? Weren't there people doing phone-sex routines like a hundred years ago?

It may be antiquated, but I understand that the human mind remains stimulated by imagery, whether that imagery is created with words or pictures.

We'll skip that part, Micah says. You sound more friendly, but your voice is still kind of bland.

Would you like to add a regional influence to my speech?

Micah thinks about this. How specific can I be?

You may select an influence as broad as a continent, or as narrow as a town or city. You may also adjust that influence by era. For example, if you prefer Victorian-era British speech, rather than twentieth century British speech, you may calibrate for such a preference.

What if you don't have the region I am interested in?

The A.I. says, I have access to a library of audio captures that are up to two hundred years old. I believe I can provide a reasonable solution if you select a region not represented in that catalog.

Okay, Micah says. Let's try California.

I have many California samples. Is there a preferred region?

Try the central coast area.

The central coast of California is available, with several further regional filters. Shall I list them?

Micah shrugs. Sure.

Monterey, California. Big Sur, California. Carmel-by-the-Sea, California. San Luis Obispo, California. Salinas, California. Santa Barbara, California. Montecito, California. San Simeon, California. Arroyo Grande, California. Morro Bay, California. Cayucos, California. Lompoc, California. Santa Cruz, California. Los Olivos, California. San--

That's enough. A lot of those areas are really close -- are you sure there's much difference between them?

Every region has a minor differentiator from the regions that surround it, the A.I. says.

Okay.

Micah visited Mae in her hometown just once, returning with her for a family reunion. She had grown up in Morro Bay, a little seaside town shadowed by a large volcanic rock. He remembered liking it very much. It reminded him of the beach house and its gray ocean and chilly skies.

Morro Bay, California, he says to the A.I.

He hears three dim tones again.

Say something, he says.

The city of Morro Bay, California, is located on a waterfront in San Luis Obispo County, the A.I. says.

Can you raise the tone of your voice? Less deepness.

Three tones.

The A.I. continues. Morro Bay's population in the early twenty-first century was --

Stop. Jesus, stop.

Micah holds his hands out and looks at his arms. His skin is covered in goosebumps. His forehead has broken out in a cool sweat.

Shall I adjust the variables --

For god's sake shut the fuck up, Micah cries.

The A.I.'s voice is eerily, horribly similar to Mae's. Micah doesn't know what he was thinking. He pushes back from the table in a hurry and walks out of the room. Over his shoulder he says, Make a new adjustment. Pick a male voice, any goddamn male voice. Adjust!

Three tones.

The A.I.'s voice is present in the living quarters, where Micah has just walked to escape the awful simulacrum of Mae that he has just created, like some sort of monster-maker.

Is this better? the A.I. asks. The voice is gravelly, deep, emphatic.

It's perfect, Micah says, pulling at his hair. Accept. It's good. Use that.

Your final selection step is to choose a name, the A.I. says. I can provide you with any naming resources you --

Bob, Micah says. Your name is Bob.

Three tones.

Bob's your uncle, the A.I. says. A joke.

Don't joke with me, Micah says.

Three tones.

Adjustment complete. Humor will not be a feature of this

selection.

Go away now, Micah says.

Very well, says the A.I., who sounds like a middle-aged smoker.

Micah goes back to the bed and wraps himself around the spare pillow again, and presses his face into its softness, and screams the longest scream he can sustain. Eyes red-rimmed and tender, pillow smushed against his cheek, he drifts into a terrible sleep.

MACHINE

Where would you like to begin? Bob asks.

Micah is standing at the window, staring down at Argus City. It is nightfall, at least until the sun rises again in ninety minutes. He doesn't know how people adjust to the frequent sunrises. Maybe their windows are timed to the station's orbital schedule, and darken each time the sun breaks like a nuclear bomb over the city.

I don't care, Micah says. Do I really have to spend twelve weeks learning this stuff?

Twelve weeks is the Earth course length, Bob says. You're already here. You can learn what you like when you like, on an as-needed or as-desired basis. Or you can simply walk the halls alone, a rogue gunslinger who doesn't need anything from anybody.

Adjust for drama, Bob, Micah grumbles.

Three tones.

What a shame, Bob says. I was good at it.

Where do you think I should start?

Bob says, Perhaps a history lesson. I can tell you how the

station fleet came to be, when the first station was constructed in orbit, and describe the current status of all twelve stations.

Let me save you some time, Micah says. We poisoned the Earth, so we built floating boats in space. The first station was built fifty years ago, and now there are twelve, and this is the coolest one.

That's fairly accurate, Bob says.

Alright, then. Let's move on.

Perhaps we should begin with the Onyx designation, Bob suggests.

Micah flaps his hands restlessly in the pockets of his bathrobe. I don't want any pop quizzes or tests, he says. Isn't there a movie or something that you could show me instead?

Do you mean an instructional video, or a dramatic film that captures the essence of the topic?

Either, I guess.

Both exist, although the instructional video is now a bit dated, and the dramatic films are usually melodramatic and feature stories of class divisions and unrequited love, Bob says.

You sound cynical, Bob.

I simply think that my summaries will prove more useful, Bob says. I can pare them down to shorter descriptions, if you like.

Short is good. I think I want to go back to sleep.

If I may, Bob says, you do sleep a --

You may not, Micah says.

Very well. Shall I begin?

Shoot.

The Onyx program, Bob begins, was created in 2182, just over a century after the first station, Station Ganymede, was deployed in high orbit. The first few years of Ganymede's progress proved interesting for sociologists, who discovered that the broad sample of humans who comprised the first space settlers were lost at sea.

Lost at sea?

Sociologically speaking, Bob says. If you recall, the first station was an experiment in class-leveling. Each person who was admitted to the first class of settlers was stripped of social status and assets. In short, each person began a new life as a perfect equal to the other settlers.

How extreme was it? Micah asks.

The most affluent member of the first settlement class was Harvey Bogleman. His personal fortune was about three hundred billion dollars when he signed up for admission. He left a small portion of the money to his family who remained on Earth, and donated the rest to the space settlement program.

That's one way to make sure you still see the benefit of your fortune, I guess, Micah says.

Indeed, Mr. Bogleman's donation accounted for approximately one-hundredth the cost of the second station, Cassiopeia. His donation, however, did not benefit him personally. He remained on Station Ganymede until his death in 2086. Having given up his privileged and wealthy status, he would have been mistaken if he had believed his donation to the program would have resulted in a better stateroom on a newer station.

Huh, Micah says. Alright, so what happened with the class experiment? It sounds like it failed.

It failed, Bob says. Sociologists concluded that humans accustomed to class perceptions found it quite difficult to shake their preconceived notions of their own status, or that of other settlers. Mr. Bogleman, in fact, fell prey to such difficulties. He was disciplined for creating an exclusive club for himself and a handful of other settlers. He called it the Harvard Club, in reference to the prestigious American institute.

So rich people still saw themselves as rich, and poor people still felt poor.

Put simply, yes. The Onyx program was created to classify future settlers in two simple categories: Onyx settlers, and Machine settlers.

Why Onyx? I mean, why was it called that.

Surprisingly, that origin story is not preserved, Bob says. I suppose someone liked the word. However, the Machine-class designation has a clearer basis.

Yeah, the escort fellow told me, Micah says. I thought it was pretty discriminatory.

On the contrary, Bob says, the purpose was to create a simple, A-B class system in order to give all settlers a clear purpose. The clearer a person's understanding of their place in the system, the theory goes, the more productive and happy they are freed to be. However, others shared your view of the program.

That it discriminates? That it's a box for second-class citizens?

The program was debated and refined by a panel of experts. A majority rule shaped the program into its final incarnation. However, two panelists resisted the program forcefully, citing a belief that it would set human progress back by a thousand years.

My kind of people, Micah says. Who were they? The two dissenters.

The first was Marshall Onlin, who originally conceived of the Onyx program. He felt that the program had been significantly changed from its initial concept, and became vocally opposed to it. The second, Bob says, was Tasneem Kyoh, a cultural anthropologist who experienced the Ganymede social experiment first-hand.

But they lost, obviously.

Obviously, Bob agrees.

So who decides who is Machine-class and who isn't? Do people buy their way into the Onyx class? It can't be that, because my wife didn't have money.

Each prospective settler is given a series of tests to identify skills. Those with extremely high intelligence markings, critical thinking skills, visionary qualities and so forth are set aside for the Onyx class. The average applicant is more suited for positions that leverage their Earth-honed talents for manufacturing, maintenance, analysis, construction, service and other industries that permit broad ranges of aptitude, Bob says.

So the smart, charismatic people get special treatment,

Micah says.

Essentially, Bob says. People with these qualities are generally quite suited for roles that benefit humanity in more resonant ways. For example, Onyx-class settlers are permitted to participate in station government and have a voice in fleet planning and futures.

I don't like this, Micah says. This sounds like you're isolating people in big buckets marked Best and Worst.

That's a simple and misinformed understanding, Bob says. Many people in the Machine class share that view.

I'm not surprised. What other privileges do Onyx people get?

Perhaps the most prominent benefit is reproductive freedom, Bob says.

Reproductive freedom? You're shitting me.

Onyx-class citizens are permitted to reproduce with other Onyx citizens at their leisure. Monogamous relationships are actively discouraged, Bob explains.

Who decided this? Micah says.

The fleet council made this a key component of the Onyx program in the fourteenth revision to the bylaws.

Fleet council, Micah says.

That's correct. The fleet council is comprised of five representatives from each of the twelve stations.

What about Machine-class citizens?

What about them? Bob asks.

What about their rights to reproduce? This is insane. I can't believe I have to ask this question.

Your questions are within the boundaries of our topic, Bob says.

That's not what I mean. I should have fucking taken that class. I shouldn't be here.

To answer your previous question, Machine-class citizens are permitted to reproduce when and if they successfully win the annual lottery, Bob says.

Micah whirls away from the window. There's a goddamn lottery?

Two hundred Machine-class citizens are permitted to reproduce annually, Bob says. The lottery is run by the station government of each individual station. Each citizen is permitted a single ticket, delivered physically to them on the first day of each year.

When do they decide who gets to have babies? Micah demands. On the last day of the year?

Indeed, Bob says.

So basically every one of these hard-working stiffs has an entire year to misplace, lose or destroy their ticket. How many people actually claim their winnings?

This lottery season, one hundred thirteen citizens claimed their reproductive authorizations, Bob says.

So eighty-seven people, probably through pure, dumb luck, don't get to start a family this year, Micah says.

Your math is correct, sir.

And how many Onyx babies were born last year?

One hundred eleven thousand four hundred seventy one,

Bob answers.

Micah turns back to the window. He pinches the bridge of his nose, thinking hard. How many Onyx citizens are there right now? he asks.

Bob says, One million two hundred eighty four thousand six hundred nine.

And how many Machine-class citizens?

Six million three hundred forty seven --

Stop, stop. I get it. You're telling me that the Onyx class is outnumbered by six to one --

That's not entirely accurate --

But it's close enough. They're outnumbered six to one, so they're having as many babies as they can, while the working class advances at a microscopic pace. So in, what -- fifteen years? -- the Onyx class outnumbers the working class altogether?

That's not entirely accurate, either.

But is that the goal? Of course my math isn't right. This is bullshit.

That is not a stated goal of the program, sir.

Onyx isn't trying to quickly grow so it can't be easily overthrown by a blue-collar riot?

No, sir.

Micah paces around the room. The sun is beginning to rise over the city again.

So what's the goal of this reproductive Nazism?

I don't believe that's an accurate term for it either, sir. But the goal is quite simple. Humanity is attempting to create successive generations of smarter, more creative and more forward-thinking people. After all, did you believe that mankind would simply relocate from Earth to Earth orbit and be satisfied with its future?

Micah stops. What are you saying?

The fleet of stations is just the first step in a very long-term plan, Bob says, to find a new home for humanity. Several, if possible.

But to manipulate the race as you go, right? Like you're breeding show dogs or racehorses.

I'm not responsible, sir. I'm simply an artificial intelligence, a companion designated to serve you.

Serve? Or observe and report?

Sir, your activities in your apartment are only recorded so that I may provide more nuanced service as I grow more informed about your preferences and requirements, Bob says.

This is bullshit, Micah says again. Bullshit.

I believe that you will find the Onyx-class life a pleasant one, sir. Onyx-class citizens are not required to hold regular positions of employment, but are provided with ample time to spend on whatever personal projects, hobbies or leisures they wish, Bob says. Onyx-class citizens have large amounts of time, and with it, they produce novels, fine artwork, political position papers, beautiful music, complex theorems and more.

But if I wanted to just sleep all day and all night, every day and night? I could do that, couldn't I.

You may spend your time however you wish, Bob says.

What if I wish to spend my time with the Machine class? What if I want to take a job, or visit a friend?

Visitations are permitted and in fact encouraged, Bob says.

But?

But Machine-class employment for Onyx-class citizens is

prohibited.

Micah paces again. Mae would never have gone for this.

It is possible that is true, Bob says.

What do you mean?

Mae Atherton-Sparrow, your deceased wife from whom you inherited your Onyx-class status, did not complete the twelve-week course. She successfully completed just under two weeks of the course.

Micah presses his palms against his eyes. And what is the curriculum for those first two weeks?

In order, Bob says, the first two weeks prepare future settlers for low-gravity transport, set packing guidelines, discuss medical waivers, allow selection of living quarters, and teach settlers about the changed day and night patterns.

When are the details of Onyx- and Machine-class policies taught? Micah asks.

On week nine, Bob says.

Week nine, Micah repeats. Mae didn't know about any of this.

It's unlikely, sir.

You know, Micah says, I didn't want to live in space. Mae did. When she died -- when she died, I was miserable for seven long, stupid years. And then one day I woke up and realized I'd let nearly a decade pass without doing anything positive. I slept all the time. I worked a shit job, and I considered becoming a drunk. But after those seven years, I suddenly wanted to do something for Mae. It took me seven years, but I wanted to honor her. So I applied for settlement. Imagine my surprise when I was not only accepted, but granted elite status.

Inheritors are truly fortunate people, Bob agrees.

No, Micah says. No. We might just be the only ones who are thinking clearly.

Micah steps out of the shower.

Bob, he says.

Yes, sir.

How exactly does a person dry off around here?

If you'll re-enter the shower, sir, I'll happily demonstrate, Bob says.

Micah opens the shower door and steps back inside.

Bob says, Any time you'd like to dry yourself, simply say the word 'dry'.

Okay, Micah says. Dry.

The shower doors hiss. Previously unseen seals tighten and pop into place. The shower becomes an isolation chamber. Micah thinks nervously about what might happen if the shower activated now. Would the chamber fill with water? Could he drown in an upright shower chamber?

Around him, dozens of tiny specks become visible in the walls. The specks form a grid pattern. Micah is reaching out to touch them when they activate. Each speck is a tiny jet. His skin ripples and rearranges itself in the blast from the miniature blasts. He feels his hair flipping about, and looks up.

Mistake. The jets in the ceiling pound his eyes, which

moisten immediately.

Try not to look at the jets, sir, Bob says.

Don't watch me in the shower, Bob, Micah says.

Three tones sound as Bob processes this. Micah imagines Bob as a tiny spook with a notepad.

Does not like it when you watch him in shower. Check.

Hello?

Mae.

I thought we agreed not to --

I'm sorry. I miss you. And it's ridiculous, not talking.

It's not ridiculous. Micah, we have a real problem.

Your boss called.

Oh.

He said that a package had arrived for you marked time-sensitive. *He wanted to know if he should have somebody messenger it over while you were on sabbatical.*

What did you say?

I said that's what he should do.

Good.

Sabbatical?

Look, I don't want to talk about it.

Are you actually in Tokyo, or did you lie about everything?

I'm in Tokyo.

Good. Okay. Why?

I told you, we're not talking right now.

I'm talking. You're not talking.

Micah, I don't need this.

This? I'm just a 'this' to you?

You know you're not.

I have tried being understanding.

You've done a bang-up job at it.

Hey. I have tried.

Micah, tell me one thing.

What?

Tell me what your single biggest dream is.

I don't know.

You know you have one. What is it?

Maybe to live in the house. And I'm doing it, so mission accomplished.

Alright. So what if I had stayed in California?

When?

Instead of moving in with you at the house. What if I had put my foot down? What if I had said you have to move to California with me, or we're through?

I -- you wouldn't have.

No, but if I had. Do you know what would have happened? I know you do. We would have broken up, Micah. Because the house is important to you. Because it holds almost an entire lifetime of meaning, and you'll never be shaken free from that. You would never want to. And I understood that, and I would never have tried to change that.

But that's exactly what you want to do now. You want to shake me free of that and take me to Pluto.

Yes, well. I do. But now it's very personal.

Why?

Because now I know that there are limits to how far you'll go to see me happy, Micah. Once you know that, you can't really go back on it.

That's such a harsh way to put it.

But it's true, Micah. It isn't a lie. It might suck to hear, but it's the truth.

Why are you in Tokyo?

It's alright. You can change the subject.

Thanks. Why are you in Tokyo?

I just am.

With somebody?

Of course not.

Because I kind of get the feeling that when you come back, everything ends. And if I have that feeling, maybe you already have that feeling, too. And maybe you figure there's no reason not to act on that feeling.

Do you realize how much we fight now? Do you think I want to come back to that?

Are you seeing somebody?

Oh, fuck you, Micah. Go back to bed.

Bob, where do I go if I want to work?

You are not required to work, sir.

Yes, I know that. But surely there are Onyx-class people who do.

Onyx-class citizens create their own jobs.

What if the job I want is not predicting social change, or writing a novel? What if I just want to push a button two thousand times a day? Or carry food to people? What if I want to run a machine press?

Bob says, You will not be permitted to have any of those jobs. Those jobs are reserved for Machine-class citizens.

Okay, what if I want to be a Machine-class citizen? Micah asks.

You can't switch your class, unfortunately, Bob answers.

No? What about Machine-class people? Can they ever become Onyx-class citizens?

Bob pauses. There are certain exceptions to the standard rule that allow for that possibility.

Oh? And what are these exceptions?

If you were to wed a Machine-class citizen, they would inherit your status as your partner, and retain your status after your death, Bob says.

That's interesting. I'm surprised that would be allowed.

Marriage of a Machine-class citizen is only permitted if the Machine-class citizen is female and expecting the child of an Onyx-class citizen, Bob clarifies.

Micah shrugs into his jacket. That's perverse, he says.

Intimate relationships between Onyx-class and Machine-class citizens require approval from Station Administration.

Micah gapes. The government permits or denies -- what the --

As I mentioned before, sir, Bob says, the Onyx program is a social experiment.

Are all twelve stations structured this way?

The Onyx program is still in its pilot phase, Bob says.

Station Argus is its proving ground.

So if there were, say, a Machine-class riot that overthrew the Onyx-class rule, this insane system wouldn't be adopted for the other eleven stations?

I suppose that's accurate, Bob says.

Huh, Micah says.

Bob says, There are protections in place to prevent such an uprising.

I'm sure. Bob, Micah says, tell me where I can get some food.

Micah leaves the apartment and rides the lift tube to the top of the petal, four hundred fifteen floors above his own. The tube is transparent and runs along a central rail of the inner petal, providing a breathtaking view of Station Argus, fully unfolded. He is transfixed by the city below, more vast than any he has ever seen. Its towers and curving transport lines turn golden in the sun's glare. From so high, the travel pods look like dewdrops on the tendril of a plant.

Micah had watched an animation on Earth that demonstrated the station's flower-like properties. The station had no stem, but its central city was flanked by ten massive petals shaped like sails. The city itself was constructed on an immense retractable platform. On days of particularly disruptive or dangerous solar flares, or if a stray asteroid ventured too close, the giant city would retract deep into the belly of the station, and the ten petals would turn and fold inward, locking together to transform Station Argus into a floating canister. Completely sealed, the station was as impenetrable as an oyster.

He shakes his head. If he'd known about the class system --

Would he still have come?

How else would he have honored Mae's memory?

Maybe another station.

But he knows that Argus is the only station currently accepting new settlers. It is the newest of the fleet, and has not yet reached its population control level.

All he had wanted was to carve out a small life, one as small as his had been on Earth, and to wake up each morning to watch the sunrise, and to have a cup of coffee and remember his wife. This new reality seems contrary to his simple goal. After just one brief conversation with Bob, Micah feels like a conspirator on the wrong side of a great and inhumane battle.

The lift carries him to the top of the petal -- at least as high as residents are permitted to visit. The observation deck -- and to his horror, restaurant and nightclub -- are still several hundred feet from the top of the tower.

A woman in a crisp dark suit meets him as he exits the lift.

Good day, sir, she says.

Hi, he says.

Seating for one? she asks.

Um, Micah says. Actually, I was just hoping to take a look from the top. If I can do that.

Of course, the woman says. You're free to move about as you choose, of course.

He nods at her as he passes, wondering if she's Machine-class. He can't imagine that the station permits Onyx-class citizens to work in the food service industry, so she must be. Is she married? Is she hoping this year for a child? What sort of work does her husband do?

Is she happy?

Micah glances back at her. She has moved back to a small, transparent podium, and is standing quite still, watching the lift indicators closely.

He feels for her. What a life.

Get it together, he thinks. *You're projecting your own feelings onto her right now. She's probably perfectly happy. She gets to live in space! No glow-in-the-dark stars pasted to the ceiling of her bedroom at night -- she gets the real thing! Where do you get off?*

The hostess turns then and smiles at him.

Get moving, Micah.

He does.

The observation platform is glorious, and terrifying. Micah is not the only person here. Several other people have already braved their fears and were floating above the city. Some are nearby, ready to return to the tower quickly if needed. Others, perhaps more daring, are quite distant and small.

Behind him is an alcove in the outer wall of the tower. This closet is filled with personal body jets, and Micah watches as a young man helps another into the suit. In fact, *suit* is the last word for the body jets. Rather, the attire is a simple exoskeleton that the wearer fits over his arms, legs, shoulders and spine. At pivot points, tiny attitude jets jut from the frame.

Excuse me, says the young man.

Micah steps back and watches as the man and his friend venture to the red line. An imprint on the floor reads:

PERSONAL GRAVITY DISABLED PAST THIS POINT
DO NOT PROCEED WITHOUT BODY JET OR TETHER

The two men walk to the red line.

Ready? the first man says.

The second man looks dubious, but he nods.

It's easy, says the first, stepping over the line.

As soon as he crosses the line, his body stops being defined by his feet. He becomes lighter, and drifts very slowly upward, following the momentum of his final footsteps. He moves his hands a bit, and Micah sees the tiny jets fire imperceptibly from his shoulders, bringing him to an almost certain halt.

The second man joins him, and after a few moments of reorienting himself, the two fire their bodyjets and sail out over the city. Micah watches them with a sense of wonder. From there, they must be able to see everything. Argus City's tallest spires are not so far below. Maybe they can even see people in the buildings.

It occurs to him then to wonder about the buildings themselves. If the million or so Onyx-class citizens don't commute to jobs there, then do only Machine-class people work there? Why would Onyx citizens need to visit the city at all? What purpose does it serve?

Again, he feels suffused with a sense of imbalance. He looks out over the station. Pale and hazy in the distance, he can see the farthest of the Onyx petals. He sees the station differently now, as though the Onyx-class citizens are on a shining hillside, looking down upon the peasants in the village.

He watches the floating people in bodyjets. They're pointing and looking below.

As if the city is a zoo, and they themselves are free.

When are you coming home?

I don't know, Micah. It's nice here, and I like it.

What are you doing with yourself?

I tour the city. I eat good food.

Are you happy?

I'm enjoying myself. But I don't know if I'm happy.

I'm not happy.

You linger over all of the things I do here. I keep wondering about us. It's turning into a scab that I can't stop scratching at.

Now I'm a scab?

You know what I mean. It's like an itch I can't scratch. Until we figure things out, it's going to be a distraction.

A distraction.

You know what I mean. Stop that.

What's that sound? Are you at a party?

I'm on a train, actually. People talk on trains.

Why are you on a train? I heard that trains in Japan are dangerous.

Not for a long time, Micah. But thank you for worrying about me. It's nice to know that you still think I can't take care of myself.

That's not what I meant, Mae.

I'm on the train back to Tokyo. I went to Kyoto for the day.

Kyoto *is* Tokyo *rearranged.*

Yeah, I hadn't thought of that before. That's nice.

You went for the day?

Yeah.

Isn't it far?

It's only an hour.

Fast train.

Yeah. Micah, I want to enjoy the view, okay. Can we talk later?

Are you coming home?

Not for a little while. There's something here I'm doing.

What are you doing?

It's nothing. I'll tell you about it another time.

I don't like this. I miss you.

We'll talk later.

Mae? I miss you.

I believe you, Micah. I'm sure you mean it.

I do.

Okay. I believe you. I'm going to go now.

Do you miss me?

Goodbye, Micah.

MAE

His last words to her made him feel ashamed. Desperate.

Do you miss me?

He didn't like the person he was then. For seven years after, he buried himself in his grief. When he was tempted to examine himself, he resisted. He learned to pretend that he wasn't really there. What he did with himself didn't matter. He gained weight, and didn't care. He went to work and home again in a haze, and didn't care. He slept often, woke up, and slept more.

One night he saw an infomercial for a neural product called the Dreambake. He didn't like the name, in fact had visions of the product actually overheating his skull until his brain became a fluffy pastry. He had never purchased anything that he had seen in an informercial before, but this time he considered it. The Dreambake was supposed to allow you to influence your dreams. It came with a manual input, allowing you to specify with startling precision the details of the dream you wanted to have, but it also had a learning feature. It would extrapolate from brain activity the deepest passions that lay dormant within your psyche, and then activate them once you slept.

He worked his shit job with Todd, a sallow-faced young man who probably only left his house to work. Todd saved his money for six months, and bought the Dreambake. With his disposable income he stocked up on sleep aids.

I literally sleep from the moment I get home from work until the moment I have to get ready for my next shift, he said to Micah one day.

Why? Micah had asked.

Because that way I can dream more, Todd confessed. It's overwhelming and it's awesome.

What do you dream about?

Different things. Sometimes I go all-in for the big spy-movie fantasies, you know. I'm running around with great clothes and hair, and I have to take out an informant before he sells his secrets to the other guy.

Todd leaned closer.

Micah leaned away.

Mostly, though, Todd had said, I dream about Erika.

Who is Erika? Micah asked.

Erika! Todd said, smacking Micah on the shoulder. Come on, man. You haven't noticed? She runs the checkout up front? Kind of girl who should be some rich asshole's trophy, not selling groceries. Erika. You know?

Micah vaguely knew who Todd was talking about. Erika, he had said.

Right. Erika! And man, let me tell you, Todd said. Let me tell you. She wouldn't talk to me at all. Said good morning to her once, and when she noticed it was me she just kept walking. It's alright, I don't blame her. I mean, look at me, Mikey.

Micah, Micah said.

Look at me. See? You get it. I get it. Hell, everybody gets it. But man, when I go home? I uploaded a photo of her into my Dreambake, see. And now she does whatever I want in my dreams.

Micah had perked up. Yeah?

See, I knew you'd come around. Best eighteen thousand dollars I ever spent. Yeah, man. Anything I want.

What if --

Naw, man. Ask. Go on. It's awesome. I don't mind telling.

What if you just wanted her to be herself? Micah had asked.

Be herself? Todd roared. Man, herself shuts me down like I'm nobody to her. Which, you know. I am. So fuck that, man. In my dream, she thinks I'm the shit. Besides, it ain't like the Dreambake knows anything about her. It just recreates her from the photo I gave it.

Could it, though? I mean, if you could tell the --

The Dreambake.

-- the Dreambake about her, could it make her actually behave like her real self?

Todd shrugs. I don't know, man. It's not like this is future tech. It is what it is. I think you pretty much have to tell it everything you want it to do, and then it does it.

Huh, Micah had said.

Man, let me tell you what she did last night, Todd went on.

Micah waved him off. No, that's alright. Please don't.

You sure?

Sure, Micah had said.

That night he had replayed the infomercial twenty times. He studied the product carefully, but nowhere among the many conversations about it online could he find the answer to his question. He posted on a forum and explained his problem, and he was swamped by messages of sympathy from strangers. But nobody could answer his question.

It wasn't a difficult question.

Will the Dreambake help me talk to my wife one last time?

He wasn't stupid. He knew it wouldn't count for anything -- that Mae was gone, and no matter what he might say to a tech toy, that would never change.

But he thought that it might make him feel a little better.

Shake him out of this nearly decade-long depression he was courting.

Eighteen thousand dollars wasn't a problem. He spent almost none of his income. He worked to forget her. His wages fell into his bank account without fanfare, day after day. He had nearly three hundred thousand dollars there, saved from years of unpacking boxes and stocking shelves.

Eighteen thousand dollars was nothing.

Hell, it cost less than eighteen thousand dollars to go to space these days.

Micah had sat up in bed at the thought.

In the morning, he resigned his position at the market.

The next afternoon, he was holding Mae's Onyx card.

I guess I can't really stop you from calling, can I.

Well, you don't have to answer.

Yes, but when it says Micah, I sort of feel like I should. I feel like it's chastising me when I don't.

Jesus, Mae. How did we end up here so fast?

I don't know. It was pretty fast, wasn't it.

I just want you to come home.

I --

Or I'll come to you. Let me come to you.

Micah, I don't know. Something doesn't feel right anymore.

Is it really just the space thing, Mae? Is there more to it?

If you're asking me that, then I think you've missed the real point, Micah.

Come home, Mae. We can work it out. I miss you.

I -- Micah, I miss you, too.

Really? Oh, this is like music. I can book a flight.

But I'm not coming home.

Mae...

I said before, I have something to do here.

What is it? Tell me what it is. I won't be upset.

Micah, I can't.

I promise. I won't be.

Okay. Promise?

I swear.

There's someone else, Micah.

He hated those dreams.

They always carried a promise of hope, sang it to him as he slept. In his dreams, Mae was hesitant, still gun-shy, but crumbling. He was gallant, willing to set aside all of his flaws, willing to consider almost anything if it meant they could be happy again.

And then the dreams took awful, terrible turns.

In them, Mae was having affairs. Sometimes just one, but in the heightened horror of Micah's dream-state, often many, simultaneously. Sometimes they were one-night stands, a quick fuck in some stranger's apartment, or worse, on the Tokyo train. Micah had heard of these things. His dreams capitalized on his fears.

But none of these things were real, and Mae didn't feel an obligation in the real world to answer his calls anymore. They went unanswered, his pleading messages unreturned.

Perhaps she was preparing him for the end, he wonders now.

If she was, she did a piss-poor job of it.

He had just come back from town.

The beach house was hazy in the fog, mostly hidden from view. He could hear the water, but couldn't see it. It was calm, almost still.

He closed the door of his Jeep, crunched across the pebbled driveway to the front door.

Mae wasn't home, of course. He missed coming home to a house that was drenched in shadow, except for the single light beside her reading chair. She wouldn't turn on more lights than she was actively using, even though the climate crisis was decades behind them and the damage long since done.

The house was empty.

He'd left the lights on.

His wrist hummed, and he looked down at the display to see a missed call. He must not have felt the tickle of an incoming call. Maybe it came while he was turning into the bumpy driveway.

He tapped the display, and in his ear, the worst message of his life unspooled, spoken by an eerily calm Japanese voice, and cross-translated by his ear tab. The message was brief -- was he the husband of Mae Atherton-Sparrow, the American space station trainee? If so, would he please return this call?

And he knew.

In the dark of his grandfather's beach house, the one he had hoped to raise children in, the one he hoped to grow very old in, the one he had so proudly introduced Mae too, the one that he had constructed his dreams around since he was a child, he knew.

Micah wakes before the first sunrise of the morning, which is scheduled to happen at 4:32 a.m. It occurs to him that, 33,000 miles above his home, his sense of time has vanished. He wonders if Station Argus is high enough above the Earth to have affected the way time works. Yes, he imagines. But he decides that nobody has rewritten the number of minutes in the day for purely nostalgic reasons.

Knowing that twenty-four/seven hasn't changed is one of the most basic comforts, he imagines, for those who have chosen to step off of the spinning ball they were raised on.

Bob says, Good morning, sir.

Micah doesn't respond. He's only sleeping in his apartment, in this bed, because he doesn't know how to access his finances. He feels strangely like a traitor, though he cannot decide whom he has betrayed. He settles on Bernard, and Mae. By accepting this privileged existence, by leaning on it, he feels as if he is being disrespectful to that kind old man and his granddaughter, and as if he is thumbing his nose at the memory of his deceased wife, who was the sweetest of souls.

If he knew how to get to his money, he'd have stayed in a hotel in Argus City last night.

He'd have looked for a place of his own.

May I recommend a breakfast selection, sir? Perhaps a coffee?

No, thank you, Micah says. Let's continue with the education selection of your programming. Tell me where I can find my bank account. And how do I shop for food?

Sir, your assets were neutralized upon entry into the Onyx system, Bob says.

Micah wishes that Bob had a face so that he could stare dumbfounded at it. I worked for most of my life to save that money, he says, finally. And it was -- neutralized?

Onyx-class citizens enjoy unfettered access to all station

systems, sir, Bob says. You will have no need for funds. To order food, simply speak your list of items, and it will be delivered to your apartment in as timely a manner as you wish. All other services are similarly free of charge.

Free, Micah repeats. I get everything for free.

Yes, sir, Bob says.

Such as?

Bob says, There are no charges or fees for your apartment or its support systems. Food is free of charge. Entertainment of all types, including physical, is free of charge. Clothing and any items you wish to purchase, including customizations for your apartment, are free of charge. Body modifications and enhancements, including neural adjustments, are free of charge.

Physical entertainment?

Physical entertainment is a polite way to describe intimate companionship, Bob explains.

Whores, then.

That is a less-polite way to describe it, sir, but you are correct.

Who chooses to be a prostitute in space? Micah wonders aloud.

Physical companionship is one of the four thousand seven hundred sixteen employment channels that Machine-class citizens are preselected for, Bob says.

Preselected, Micah repeats. You mean, the government taps new arrivals and says, You're a ship mechanic, you're a bartender, you're a gardener, you're a... piece of meat?

Machine-class citizens are invited to submit their qualifications for their preferred positions, Bob says. Physical companions often select that line of employment for themselves. I believe the consensus is that it is less physically-taxing than other Machine-class employment positions, and therefore, in some segments of the population, a desired position. Like other more interesting employment positions, physical companionship is one option with a waiting list.

Micah shakes his head. Okay, I can't think about that anymore.

As you wish, sir.

So the things that are free to me, Micah says. Are those only things I can get in the tower here?

No, sir, Bob says. Services that are free to you can be found all over Station Argus, both in the towers and in Argus City.

So I could go to the city today and buy a sandwich.

Of course, sir. At no cost to you.

I could buy a new wardrobe.

Yes, sir. At no cost.

I could visit the holopark.

Yes, sir, Bob repeats. At no cost.

I could... stay in a hotel?

In theory, sir. I would be remiss not to instruct you that sleeping out-of-quarters will raise an alert that you did not return to your apartment.

An alert. You mean someone tracks me.

I track you, sir, Bob says.

Stop tracking me, Bob.

I'm not at liberty to do so, sir. Personal tracking is less invasive than you may think. I simply observe your activities in order to better serve you.

So if I didn't come home --

In that case, sir, I am required to submit an alert to station government.

You have to tell *the government* if I don't come home at night? Jesus.

I am required to inform the station government, sir, and when you return to your apartment, you would be contacted by an administrator. The administrator would be charged with ascertaining why you did not return to your quarters at night.

Jesus fuck, Micah says. Why is that anybody's business but my own?

Absence from your apartment can be an indicator of several scenarios that the government must monitor, sir, Bob says. For example, it may indicate that you have begun a physical relationship with a Machine-class citizen.

Which is the government's business *why*?

Such a relationship may lead to complexities regarding that Machine-class citizen's status. If that citizen were impregnated, for example, without administration approval --

Holy shit, Micah says. I don't want to hear this.

-- then protocol regarding said pregnancy would go into effect.

You're talking about abortion. You're talking about forced government-sponsored abortion. Population control.

No, sir. Not strictly population control. Unauthorized class expansion is taken quite seriously. As I mentioned before, Onyx-class citizens are welcomed and even encouraged to reproduce among themselves as frequently as they like.

This is one goddamn horrible experiment you're running on this station, Bob.

I am simply your apartment's artificial intelligence, sir.

We'll see about that, Micah said.

He pulled on his clothes, threw open the door, and stomped into the hallway, still pulling on his coat.

Bob closed the door behind him.

What did you think when you first saw me?

We've talked about this before, haven't we?

Tell me again.

Well, I thought there was no one more beautiful in the whole world.

And you wanted to marry me right then and there.

I wanted to marry you a thousand times in one day.

And you wanted lots of babies.

All of the babies.

Did you think, wow, check out that bod.

I didn't.

Not even a little bit? I'm sad.

I really didn't. I was captivated just watching you smile and laugh.

You didn't even notice my butt? I have a very nice butt.

You were standing behind that food cart. I couldn't see your butt.

Ah, so you tried.

I didn't. But I'm sure if I had seen your butt, I really would have liked it.

You're a pervert.

I remember thinking, I bet she looks this amazing in any light. Because it was a very lovely morning, and the sun was shining through your hair and doing that thing where it makes you almost glow. And I thought, you probably glow at night, in the dark.

Like a radioactive princess.

My radioactive princess.

Micah.

Yes.

I'm sorry.

Sorry? What for?

For all of this. Look around. It's not what I wanted.

It's kind of scary, isn't it.

I wanted to have babies in in space, in the glow of a star, to make them shine and then push them out into the dark and let them light up the universe.

You're such a romantic.

I wanted to huddle together with you over a space campfire, all of the darkness around us, and know that we were special, we were together, we were the only two people for a hundred million trillion miles.

And instead, it's terrifying.

I don't even feel like I know who human beings are anymore.

They say it's an experiment, Mae.

It's a horrible one. You thought that the lower-class citizens were like animals in a zoo, but you were wrong. You all are.

The thought occurred to me.

What are you going to do?

I don't know. I could start a revolution.

I bet a lot of people have tried that.

You think?

It's scary how much they know about you already.

They probably know I'm not feeling their little utopia, I guess.

Not feeling it at all.

In fact, they're probably watching me right now.

Watching you sleep? Probably.

Is that what I'm doing? Sleeping?

You thought there was another way we could be talking?

I didn't buy the Dreambake.

Good. Infomercial products are garbage. It probably would kill all of your brain cells at one time.

But this is the conversation that I would have dreamed of if I had.

Maybe.

Maybe?

You weren't living in an oppressive cage at the time.

You could argue that my grief was a cage.

Yes, but you made that cage.

I was oppressing myself.

You were sad, Micah.

I was sad.

I know. If it had been different, I would have been sad, too.

I couldn't believe that you were gone. And that I wasn't with you when it happened.

I'm sorry.

I'm sorry, too.

What are you going to do now, Micah?

Probably not start a revolution. I don't think I'd be very good at it.

You could marry again. Have space babies.

I can't even think about that. I don't look at women like that. Nobody is you.

They don't have to be me. They just have to make you happy.

They don't.

What does?

I don't know. The beach house didn't even work after you died.

You haven't been happy in seven years?
Seven years and one terrible argument.
That's awful, Micah. It's my fault.
It's mine, too.
So we're both responsible for your life being tragic.
Yes, I guess so.
Chivalrous of you to take all of the responsibility.
Hey, you did kind of run away to Tokyo.
I did. So I guess you're right, it's kind of my fault, too.
I'll settle for that.
So. What will you do?

Argus City dazzles in the darkness. Constellations of light, the flicker of pods darting between the spires. Sparkling towers constructed from seamless transparent steel catch the moonlight and throw it around like fine china that splinters and turns.

Micah is alone tonight.

It's not even night. It's two in the afternoon, but the sun has dropped behind the Earth, and only the faintest golden glow breaks the planet's crisp horizon line.

If he closes his eyes, can almost convince himself that he's still on Earth. His ears reproduce the soft, papery surge of the waves. He can feel the damp wood planks of the pier beneath his feet. He remembers the most important voices that he ever heard in exactly that spot. His grandfather's, telling him that one day they would build a boat together, and that if it sank, then they would build a ship in a bottle instead.

And Mae's, closer, her breath on his neck, simply saying good morning.

Mae.

Mae.

Micah fits his arms into the bodyjet, and steps back, clicking his feet into the heel clips. The exoskeleton feels kind of nice against his limbs. A cradle for his fragile human body, perhaps.

What does one say in a moment such as this one?

He settles for nothing at all.

What did you think? When you first saw me?

That you were the most handsome man I had ever seen.

Bullshit. You didn't think that at all.

You're right.

Am I? Damn. I don't like being right.

You're right. I didn't think anything, because you put my brain into a coma.

That was pretty mean of me.

Oh, I don't know. It's been a fine coma-dream.

The finest, Mae.

I miss you.

I love you.

Micah steps across the red line.

He hangs there, suspended, just a couple of feet from the safety and artificial gravity of the observation deck.

I could go back, he thinks.

He looks down. The great petal narrows as it falls away beneath him. Hundreds of windows, some of them dimmed, most glowing with activity. He wonders if anybody is looking outside, looking up. Does anybody see him up here?

The city swims away beneath him, bursting with activity.

The zoo.

He glances back at the observation deck and is startled to see a face in the window. It belongs to the hostess from a few days ago. He meets her gaze, and she lifts a hand. He offers a smile.

She looks upward, at the blackness beyond the ring of petals.

He follows her gaze. The ten towers, like points of a crown. The doorway to beyond that exists between them.

The hostess smiles back, and waves once more. Then she turns from the window and is gone.

Mae, Micah thinks.

He fires the tiny attitude jets, turning his back to the tower.

The sun is beginning to rise.

He turns his face into its warmth, fires the jets, and rises with it.

Argus City recedes.
Micah approaches, and then passes the ring of petals.
The sun is warm, but everything else is so cold.
Mae.

BERNARD

His closet is full of sweaters.

There's one of almost every color, one for almost every year of a fifty-year marriage.

Some are scratchy. Some are silky-smooth. Some don't fit so well. Some feel like home.

Bernard's sweaters are a metaphor for his marriage.

There hasn't been a new sweater in six years.

He hates today.

Today he must choose one sweater.

He'll wear that sweater for the rest of his life.

Angelika waits for him to come to her bedroom each

morning. He tells her that she can get up and play, or pour a bowl of cereal, that she doesn't have to wait for him, but she does. He reminds himself that she has lost more than he has, and comes to her room each morning with a smile and kind eyes.

This morning she is sitting up in bed. Clutched in her arms is a stuffed dragon with googly eyes. She calls the dragon Sir Patrick, but Bernard doesn't know why.

Good morning, Angelika, he says.

She doesn't say anything, but then, she hasn't spoken in months.

He holds out his hand.

Angelika climbs down from the bed. She is so small in her nightgown.

She takes his hand, and they go downstairs.

Do you remember what today is? he asks.

Angelika sits at the enormous table and stares at Sir Patrick. She doesn't answer.

Bernard scrambles some eggs. Today, he says, is the day you and I go on a trip together.

Still nothing from the little girl.

Bernard stands back from the stovetop and looks at the kitchen. The cabinets that he restored twenty years ago are in need of restoration again. He was never much of a carpenter to begin with.

He closes his eyes. He can still imagine Marguerite chiding him.

These doors, they barely close, she would say.

I did the best I could, he would reply.

Oh, I know you did. But couldn't you have done a little better? It's I who has to use them every day.

He misses her.

The new settlers, unlike the first hundred waves, are permitted small bags of things. Space is precious and finite aboard Station Argus, he is told, though he has seen photographs and videos that prove it is the most vast of palaces

He packs Angelika's bag with her clothing and shoes and books.

As he puts things into her bag, he says, Angelika, is this important to bring?

But she would only look at him with her big, sad eyes.

In the end, he packed her bag with all he could, and then packed his own with more of her things.

For himself, he packs only a rubber-banded stack of letters that Marguerite wrote to him when he was in the war, years and years and years before. He smiles at the idea that she would spritz the paper with her perfume before she mailed them to her. He has sniffed at them so often that the scent is gone. But still he breathes deeply whenever he opens them.

Angelika still bears a fine scar on her brow from the day she stopped speaking. Each time she looks at Bernard, he is reminded of the day. He had collected her from the hospital.

Angelika and her parents, Jared and Sara -- Bernard's daughter -- had been admitted together.

Days later, Angelika had been discharged into Bernard's custody, alone.

He did not attend the funeral. Angelika was barely sleeping, and though she did not speak, she was distraught. He felt if he left her, she would implode. And to carry her to the funeral was beyond consideration.

So Bernard missed his daughter's burial ceremony.

The house felt somehow emptier afterward, as though all of the memories that Sara had created within its walls had been sucked away at the moment of her burial. He missed the sounds of her laughter and footsteps, the shadow of her ballet routines cast on the wall by the living room fireplace.

For a few weeks, he slept on a bed roll on the floor beside Angelika's bed. He wanted to be there when she woke, upset. Eventually she slept through the night without interruption, but Bernard still lay on the floor, awake well into the night.

He had wished to move to a smaller house in recent years, now that Sara was grown and moved away, and with a baby of her own. But Marguerite would not hear of it.

This home is my skin now, she had said to him. *It's my happiness, my nest. I won't leave it.*

It's so big, he had argued. It's bigger than we need. And we can't keep up with all of the repairs forever.

But she would not discuss it more after that, and he had finally let it go.

He is grateful now for this. He cannot imagine enduring life now in a strange place, one with carefully-painted walls and cabinets that don't stick or jerk around.

In the morning, he and Angelika will travel.

He peeks into her room and sees that she is asleep. Sir Patrick has fallen to the floor.

Bernard creeps across the creaking floor and puts the toy dragon on the pillow beside her.

Angelika sighs in her sleep.

Angelika, he says. Do you have your bag?

She walks over to the hallway and points. He looks down

the hall and sees her bag resting beside the door.

Okay, he says. Are we forgetting anything?

She just looks up at him, then points.

He looks down.

Right, he says. My sweater.

Angelika follows him up the stairs, then leans in his bedroom doorway and watches.

He stands before the closet, at a loss.

There's the beige sweater that Marguerite made for him before he shipped overseas. Or the soft blue one that she knitted in front of the downstairs fireplace for their tenth anniversary. There's the sad rust-colored one that he wore when he found her in her chair, cold and peaceful. And there's the green one that she made for their first real family vacation. He had worn it in Hawaii despite the heat.

My traveling sweater, he had called it.

Bernard picks up the hanger and turns to Angelika. He holds the sweater up and raises his eyebrows.

Angelika studies it, then nods once.

Bernard carefully removes the sweater from the hanger and pulls it on. He replaces the hanger in the closet, then runs his hands over the remaining sweaters. He gathers them in his arms, draws them tight. He tries to hold the sob deep inside so that Angelika won't hear it, but he fails.

He feels her small hands encircle his leg.

Bernard cries and cries and cries.

He is the oldest man aboard the shuttle.

Even now, over a century after the first settlers fled Earth, citizens over the age of fifty are not permitted to migrate. Angelika, in this case, is Bernard's saving grace. She has inherited her parents' settlement rights, but as an orphan, she cannot migrate without a guardian.

Bernard slips through the loophole.

The shuttle traces a golden path through the sky like a sparkler.

Angelika attends a school in the fourth district of Argus City, and Bernard is assigned employment there as well. He is grateful for this closeness. He cannot bear the idea of Angelika being whisked away each day while he, at his age, travels equally far to put items into boxes for hours and hours.

Instead, he stands in the school's cafeteria, watching children eat lunch, and intervening when childhood warfare erupts. He is happy that the children are generally well-behaved. His diplomacy skills have rusted in the years since Sara was a child.

The days are repetitive, and Bernard settles into the routine with groaning bones and tired hands. Soon he will be too old for this, and what of Angelika then? He worries daily about her future. When he dies, what will happen to her?

Machine-class residents have little control over these things.

Bernard wakes to a thumping at the door. Angelika is at his side, pulling at his hand. When she sees that he is awake, she points at the door to their quarters.

He nods. I'm awake, child.

He makes his way across their small home to the door.

Who is it? he asks.

Courier, comes the reply.

Angelika retreats into the corner of the room and sinks to the floor. She hasn't grown accustomed to people visiting their home yet.

Bernard opens the door a sliver and leans into the gap.

The woman outside says, Congratulations, sir, and hands Bernard a slim package in metallic charcoal-colored paper.

What is it? he asks.

Turn it over, she says.

He does. Embossed on the paper is a single word:

ONYX

I don't understand, he says.

The courier says, I deliver maybe one of these every six months. Don't question it.

But what is it?

You should open it, sir, the courier says, and walks away.

Bernard carries the package to the dining table and sits down.

Angelika comes over. She looks at the package questioningly.

Bernard holds it up, turns it over, shows her the embossed label.

She looks at him with the same question in her eyes.

I don't know, he says.

His fingers seem to be trembling.

Inside are three objects.

The first is a small, silvery card.

Bernard inhales sharply.

He turns the card over. There's an empty rectangle printed on the surface, but nothing else.

He looks at Angelika. Her curiosity is apparent.

He presses his thumb against the rectangle.

The card shimmers to life, revealing an identity profile.

Micah Roderick Sparrow
0627J007-1211-E
H 5'11" W 192

Bernard says, Oh, my.

He shows the card to Angelika, who betrays no recognition.

Do you remember? Bernard asks. We met this man on the shuttle. He tried to give me this card then.

Angelika shakes her head.

Right, Bernard says. I had forgotten that you were asleep. Well, this man was there with us. He wanted to give me his card, but the authorities wouldn't let him do it.

Angelika just looks at him with big eyes.

Bernard smiles, then touches the rectangle on the card again.

Micah's profile shimmers away, replaced by a single red line of text:

Deceased September 12, 2185

Bernard gasps and drops the card.

Angelika jumps.

My god, Bernard says. He stares at the card as if it were a weapon. Then, carefully, he picks it up again.

He stares at those words.

Deceased September 12, 2185

Oh, that poor man, Bernard whispers.

Angelika points at the rectangle, which is pulsing gently.

Bernard sighs, and presses his thumb to the card.

Micah's epitaph vanishes, replaced with a new profile.

Bernard Samuel Hinske

1244M943-8920-R

H 5'9" W 164

Bernard has no words.

He stares at the card for a long time. His own photograph stares back with warm, tired old eyes. Then he remembers the other objects in the box.

The second item is a silvery booklet. The cover reads

Welcome to the ONYX Program

Bernard opens it briefly, sees the mountain of words inside, and closes it again.

Angelika reaches across the table for the third item, then looks up at Bernard.

He nods. It's okay.

The final item is a square of pale yellow paper. Angelika unfolds it, reads its contents, then holds it up to Bernard.

He lifts Angelika into his lap, then reads the paper as well.

Bernard:

I won't have any use for this any more. Missing her was too much, and some things here are too dark.

You, my friend, deserve to raise that little girl in the light.

Please make the most of that.

Micah

Bernard closes his eyes.

Angelika looks toward the front door a moment before the knock comes.

Gather your things, my dear, Bernard says.

And he opens the door.

NATHAN

Anya studies her reflection in the glass table top. She likes the way her eyes look today, her eyeliner swept outward, as if her eyes are white-hot, leaving vapor trails when she moves. She tilts her head forward, looks up at herself from beneath her dark brow.

Smoky, Nathan says, returning to the table.

You think?

I do.

Nathan slides into the booth across from Anya.

Smoky, she repeats.

No food, Nathan observes.

Not yet, she says.

I always thought that using the restroom while you wait for your food was sort of like a cosmic guarantee that when you returned, your food would be hot and ready and waiting for you.

Anya spreads her hands over the table. If you ordered the

242

imaginary rice curry, then you are correct. But if you didn't, you're just delusional.

Delusional! Nathan laughs.

Delusional, Anya says. I, however, have already received and finished my food while you were locked away in the bathroom, powdering your nose.

My nose never needs powder, Nathan says.

Anya smiles. No, you're right. Your nose is perfect.

So, Nathan says, folding his hands. What are we doing today? I heard that there's a movie festival.

Good movies? Anya asks.

Nathan shrugs. Probably pretentious movies. Or terrible ones. Aren't all festivals that way?

I thought we could visit the Japanese gardens.

There's an idea, Nathan says. A stroll beneath the maples and cherry blossoms.

The sun is up for another two hours, Anya says. Maybe it will go down while we are in the garden. Like last time.

What happened last time? a woman asks, sliding into the booth next to Anya. The stranger is almond-skinned, with short, dark hair. The narrow stripe of gray in her hair catches Anya's eye, and her first thought is, Jesus, that's very cool.

Anya's next thought, which she says aloud, is: What are you doing?

I thought I'd join you for lunch, the stranger says. Seeing as you're still waiting, I should order.

The stranger drags her finger across the surface of the table, and quickly taps an item from the menu that swims into view.

There, she says. A cheese sandwich. What were you two having?

Nathan leans across the table. Alright, who the hell are you?

We're having a private lunch, Anya adds.

The stranger smiles calmly.

Anya is taken by the stranger's eyes, which seem almost golden in the light. Then the stranger turns and looks directly at her, and Anya realizes that her eyes are a pale green.

Private lunches in public places, the stranger observes. What a quaint notion.

I'm going to report this, Nathan says, reaching for his wrist.

The stranger cocks her head to the side, as if she's listening to someone that Anya can't hear.

Then she says, I'd rather you didn't -- Matthew.

Nathan stops cold.

His name is Nathan, Anya says. That's all this is, then. You've just got the wrong table.

The stranger doesn't take her eyes off of Nathan.

No, she says. This is most certainly the correct table.

Anya turns to Nathan. You're sweating, she says. Nathan? Are you alright?

What do you want? Nathan asks.

The stranger smiles, and this time her smile is genuine, almost friendly. She holds her hand out, and Nathan stares at it, confused.

I'm Tasneem, the stranger says. And I have a proposition for you, Mr. Bogleman.

The Japanese gardens occupy a generous portion of real estate on the eastern border of Argus City, a lush green scrawl of land that curves between the city's smaller towers. The land is domed, its personal atmosphere carefully monitored. Thousands of Argus residents filter through the park each week. Humans may have claimed space as their new frontier, but they still crave the Earth.

Wait, wait, Anya says, struggling with the conversation.

Tasneem stops and turns back. Yes, Miss Basura?

Nathan has been strolling next to Tasneem Kyoh, hands in his pockets, brow furrowed, shoulders bowed under a new weight.

I'm still -- I --

Tasneem turns to Nathan. I believe she's struggling with your deception.

You're a Bogleman! Anya spits out. Why didn't you tell me?

Nathan's eyes are sad. Why would I tell you? That's not who I am.

Anya says, You tell me because I'm your partner, Nathan. You tell me because we don't lie to each other.

Nathan Gerard is my name, Nathan says. It wasn't a lie. It isn't.

It's a stage name, Anya says. It's a costume.

Yes, Nathan says. That's exactly what it is. A mask.

Anya stomps one foot on the pebble path. You *tell* me these things, Nathan.

Tasneem looks on, amused, as Nathan goes to Anya.

Sweetheart, Nathan says. He takes her hands. Anya. Look at me.

Anya looks at the ground.

Anya, Nathan repeats.

She looks up reluctantly.

My grandfather was a very rich man, Nathan says. On Earth, he threw his money around like a battle axe. When he moved to space, he had to give up the money, so he learned to throw his influence around instead. He wasn't a nice man. He wasn't evil, but he wasn't kind. He believed in the elite class. He believed in privilege.

Tasneem walks to a bench and sits down. She tilts her head again as if listening to someone who isn't there.

Who cares about your grandfather, Anya says.

My grandfather invented the Harvard Club, Nathan says.

Anya's eyes widen.

For my grandfather, it was simply a boys' club, he continues. He and other formerly rich men would gather in secret, share alcohol that they'd skimmed from station resources, and tell stories of their glory days. I'm sure they had ideas of overturning the class-leveling system of Ganymede -- they probably *hated* being considered the equals of working-class residents -- but to my knowledge they never did much more than bitch and moan about it.

Nathan exhales heavily. If it had stopped there, it would have been fine. The Harvard Club was just a bunch of crabby old men. It wasn't what you know it as. In fact, it died with my grandfather. The club disbanded.

Tasneem says, Nathan's father was William Bogleman.

Anya shakes her head. William Bogleman was childless. That's why he was able to be so --

So ruthless, Tasneem finishes. That was a fabrication. William had six children, each with different mothers. Nathan

246

here is the last of the brood. The runt, so to speak.

Anya turns to Nathan. You have brothers and sisters? You told me you were an only child.

I am, he says. They're all dead. And I never knew them, anyway.

William's children were murdered, Tasneem says.

Anya gasps.

Nathan looks down at his feet.

They were murdered by enemies that William made when he resurrected the Harvard Club and turned it into a criminal organization, Tasneem says. William's children were delivered to him in pieces. It was quite gruesome.

Nathan nods. I changed my name. Well, my mother changed it for me.

She was murdered, too, Tasneem says. When she wouldn't give her son up, she was walked to a shuttle dock. They put her into an airlock. Then they opened the door, but only a couple of inches.

Anya claps her hands to her mouth. My god, she says.

Nathan's mother was --

Stop, Nathan says. Jesus Christ.

Tasneem nods. So your boyfriend has a new identity. I don't know if you can tell, but he's had some reconstructive treatments. That's not his nose, for one.

Anya's eyes are damp.

Nathan says, I'm sorry I couldn't tell you.

Anya shakes her head. I -- you -- Nathan, I --

It's okay, he says.

Anya steps into his arms. Nathan looks over her shoulder at Tasneem.

What do you want, really? he asks.

Tasneem says, What do you know about David Dewbury?

In here, Tasneem says.

She leads Anya and Nathan into a narrow space between two towers in the Gaia District. Tasneem presses her palm against a sheer wall, and it shimmers and becomes transparent. Inside, Anya can see modest living quarters -- a simple bed, a table and chair, a basic kitchen module.

A segment of the wall slides open.

Please, Tasneem says.

Anya follows Nathan inside, and can instantly see that the living quarters are only one small piece of a larger facility.

What is this place? she asks.

Tasneem enters behind her. The wall slides closed again. She presses her palm against it, and it becomes opaque, invisible from the slim alley outside.

This, Tasneem says, is your war room.

Anya looks confused. I don't understand.

Nathan says, You have to tell me what you want, right now, or we're leaving.

I agree, Tasneem says. Please. Sit.

David Dewbury, Tasneem says again. What do you know?

Anya says, I learned about him in school. A few years ago.

Tasneem nods. Nathan?

My father killed him, Nathan says. It was what led to the breakdown of the Harvard Club.

David Dewbury was a beloved thinker, Tasneem explains. If you put him in a room of astrophysicists, he would dazzle and confound them. If he were among a party of theologians, he would have them proclaiming that the god myth was over. He was the sort of man for whom *genius* was too shallow a word.

And your father killed him? Anya says.

David wanted the Soma treatment, Tasneem continues. But he couldn't have it. Nathan, you know why.

Everybody knows why, Nathan says. The man's a sort of cult figure now.

Why? Anya asks. I can't remember.

He killed his parents, Nathan says. He was a prodigy, and his parents were drunks and addicts. They would lock him in closets, or tie him to furniture. They treated him like an animal because --

-- because they didn't understand him, Anya finishes. I remember now.

When people applied for Soma, Tasneem says, they were subjected to weeks of careful examination. If you failed even a tiny component of the exam, you were denied treatment.

David knew he would never pass muster, no matter how vital his mind was to mankind.

He took Amrita instead, Nathan says.

Holy shit, Anya breathes. And your father --

My father ran the black market for it on Aries, Nathan says. All told, nearly seventy people died from Amrita. Nobody survived it.

Anya turns to Tasneem. This is terrible, but why the history lesson? What does it matter?

Tasneem says, Watch.

Tasneem removes a wristband from her left arm and places it on a depression in the table. The table begins to glow.

Nathan, do you mind? Tasneem says, pointing.

Nathan follows her gaze to a square button. This?

Tasneem nods. Press it, please.

Nathan does.

A seam in the ceiling opens, and a tiny projector descends. A few feet away, two more appear. There is a rainbow flare of light, and the three projectors shine down upon the table. A pale hologram rises from the light, and gains substance as the lights begin to flicker more quickly.

Anya, Nathan, Tasneem says. I'd like you to meet David Dewbury.

Anya stares in wonder. It's like watching an old movie.

It's not a movie, Tasneem says. Otherwise I'd agree with

you.

What is it? Nathan asks.

It's David, Tasneem says. Say hello, David.

The holographic figure bows modestly. Hello, it says.

Oh, my, Anya says.

How? Nathan asks.

It's not terribly important how, Tasneem says. David, would you like to take it from here?

The figure sits down on the table and folds its legs, one over the other.

Sure, David says. Pardon my appearance, please. It's not a perfect representation, but it's what I have to work with. Nathan, I'd like to answer your question -- what does Tasneem want from you? It's a bigger question than that, though. You might also ask what I want from you. But it's bigger than that, still. Do you know what the question is?

Nathan shakes his head.

Anya? David asks.

Anya says, What does history want from him?

That's a very nice way of putting it, Tasneem says.

I agree, David says.

What do you mean, history? Nathan asks.

You are each Machine-class citizens, correct? David asks.

We are, Nathan says.

What history requires is quite simple, David says. Tasneem?

Tasneem leans forward and looks Nathan in the eye, then Anya.

We want you to overthrow Station Administration, Tasneem says. We want you to bring down the Onyx program.

Anya is stunned.

Nathan jumps up. There's no way, he says. Let us out.

David says, Nathan. You've run from your name for a very long time. Wouldn't you like to reclaim it, and redeem it?

Fuck, no, Nathan says. My new name serves me fine. I have no loyalties to the Bogleman line.

You're happy with your status as a second-rate citizen, then, Tasneem says.

Perfectly happy, Nathan says. Keeps me out of sight. It's easy to hide.

And you'd like to continue hiding, Tasneem says.

Damn straight, Nathan says.

And you, Anya? Are you content with a life such as that?

Anya bites her lip. I don't know, she says.

When he returns home late from work, Tasneem says, you'll worry. Was this the day he was found out?

Leave her alone, Nathan says. What good does it to me to go public? Then I'm just a target for anybody who remembers my father and his crimes.

People still love a good story, Tasneem says. Especially a redemption story.

It's not that easy, Nathan says.

It actually is, David replies. Of course, we'll provide you with some protection, but we expect that a well-placed rumor or two would lead to a groundswell of opinion reversal. Not to mention a rise in your ranks.

Nathan shakes his head. I'm not a revolutionary, he says. The system works just fine.

The system says that you and Anya can't have children until the government says so, Tasneem says. Anya? Do you want children?

Anya looks at Nathan. We've never talked about it, but --

There's no use getting her hopes up, Nathan snaps.

-- but I hope every year that we're one of the few, Anya finishes.

Nathan stops and looks at her. You never told me that.

It seemed foolish, Anya says. Only a few hundred people are even allowed the chance. It would probably never, ever be us.

Have you heard of Meili? Tasneem asks.

Meili is a myth, Nathan says.

I assure you, Meili is real, David interjects.

What is Meili? Anya asks, looking back and forth.

Meili is the next space station, Nathan says. It's a rumor.

Meili construction is underway, David says. I've been following its progress religiously.

Tasneem says, It's planned as a second Onyx station.

Station Argus's social experiment has proven so successful, David says, that Meili will be structured in the same way. There is talk of rolling the program backwards across the other stations as well.

Nathan stops pacing. They can't do that.

Anya says, What does that mean?

Tasneem levels her gaze at the two young people and says, It means that from here on, forever, the Egyptians will whip the Israelites until their backs are bloody and they die in the trenches. It means that you, and your children, if you are so fortunate as to be allowed to reproduce, will be slaves. Forever.

You see, this isn't just about you, Anya, David says. It isn't just about you, Nathan. If the Machine-class people of Station Argus do not rebel and claim the freedom and expression that is rightfully theirs, then almost all of humanity will join you as subservient members of a once-free society.

It won't pass, Nathan says, weakly. One of the stations will revolt. They won't just take it.

Do you want to count on that? Tasneem asks.

Anya says, Nathan --

Nathan explodes. Why me? Why not someone else?

Tasneem says, You're Matthew Bogleman. Who better to lead the revolution?

David says, Will you? Will you help us?

Anya looks at Nathan balefully.

I need time to think about it, Nathan says.

You don't have time, Tasneem says. I'm deeply sorry about that, but this must begin now.

Anya says, Nathan. I want to have a baby.

Nathan looks at Anya, then closes his eyes. I don't want to do this, he says, finally.

What is right often has nothing to do with what you want, David offers.

Tasneem folds her arms. Well?

What if you're both wrong? Nathan asks. What if Onyx never goes any farther than this station?

Then congratulations, Tasneem says. You're both members of the most discriminated-against group of human beings in the fleet. Nathan, if you don't want to do this, you don't have to. We'll find someone else.

Either way, David adds, there will be a revolution.

You can lead it, Tasneem says, or you can be swept up by it. And I have a feeling that as much as you're pushing against us, you aren't really the follower type. I think you've got a bit of your grandfather in you.

Like him or not, David says, he refused to be marginalized.

Anya squeezes Nathan's hand. Nathan, she says.

Nathan's shoulders slump. Alright, he says.

Tasneem claps her hands and hops to her feet. She picks up the wristband from the table, and David's image vanishes.

Good, she says. Follow me. There are people for you to meet.

Anya stands up. Can we have a moment first? Please?

Tasneem looks at the two of them. They suddenly look very small. The last thing that anybody would mistake Nathan for would be a revolutionary.

Of course, she says. I'll be outside.

Well? she thinks.

I think he's weak, David says.

Do you think he can win?

I think it doesn't matter if he wins, David says. *All you need is to turn public opinion. If he fails, someone else will rise up. You'll have planted a weed.*

Weeds are good, Tasneem says.

The door opens, and Anya pushes Nathan forward.

Anya says, Go on, tell them.

Nathan looks almost sheepish. It's just -- I --

He doesn't know how to start a revolution, she says. You can teach him, right?

Nathan looks down at his feet.

Tasneem steps forward and puts her hands on Nathan's shoulders.

We can teach you everything, she says. First thing's first -- you need a first mate. Who do you trust?

Nathan doesn't hesitate. Eldon, he says. Eldon Heave. He'll do anything for me.

He's loyal? Tasneem asks.

Completely, Nathan says. As am I, to him.

That's where we start, then, she says. Let's go.

ZITA

She called again, didn't she.

He stops fumbling in the closet in the dark. I didn't know you were awake. I was trying not to wake you.

But she did, didn't she.

Yeah. Yeah, Zita, she did.

Zita says, Lights.

The bedroom illuminates.

Well, what does she need this time? Zita asks.

I'm not sure, he answers.

Why does she call you? The station has people for these things.

I don't know. You know how the repair team is, he says. They take a pretty long time.

What are you looking for?

He is shoulder-deep in the closet.

Zeke, she says.

Huh?

What are you looking for?

Zeke steps back and plants his hands on his waist. Huh, he says. I was looking for my shoes.

They're under the bed, Zita says.

Zeke kneels down. They're under the bed, he says.

He fishes them out, then sits on the edge of the bed to put them on.

You don't want to know why they were under the bed? Zita asks.

Zeke shrugs. I guess I put them there. I just forgot.

Zita scoots across the bed and whacks Zeke's head. No, you idiot. I put them there. Don't you want to know why?

I guess, Zeke says, rubbing his head.

Because, Zita says.

Okay.

She snakes an arm around his chest.

Because, she says again.

Because why?

Because I don't want you to go to her, Zita says.

Zita, honey --

No, don't take that tone, she says. You're not going to her. You're staying here with me.

Zita slides her hand down his chest.

Zita, come on. You know I have to go.

She sits back on her knees and pulls the blanket around her. You do not, she says.

If I don't go, she'll just call again. You know that.

That's no reason to go running off to her.

You say it like she's some slinky thing, Zeke says.

Zita doesn't answer.

She's not some slinky thing, Zeke says. She's your sister.

Even more reason, Zita says, but she senses that she is losing the argument.

She needs help now that Arnan's gone, Zeke says.

Arnan, Zita says. If you'd asked me a year ago, could Arnan be any worse than he already is? I'd have said no. But then he up and left her with those little ones.

You're making my argument for me, Zeke says.

Zeke, please don't go. She'll be fine. I'm sure it's just a broken switch or something.

If it is, she could freeze to death, Zeke says.

She won't freeze to death.

She might, he says. We've got it okay here on Tycho. I mean, it's no Argus, but Galileo is a shit station, and you know it. It's like an old automobile somebody crashed in the woods and let the battery run out. If she's got a climate problem and nobody fixes it, her compartment will have icicles by morning.

Well, then I'm coming with you, Zita says.

Zita, he says.

It's final, Zeke.

Zita, it's a long trip. I'm just going to sleep in the orbital on the way there, and sleep on the way back, and then I'm going straight to work. There's no point.

Zeke, she says weakly.

You have nothing to worry about, he says, taking her hands in his.

I don't trust --

I know, he says. But there's nothing to worry about. She's your sister. And I'm your husband, for Pete's sake.

She's cunning, Zita says.

I'm impervious to cunning, he says.

Stay here?

He shakes his head. Look, I don't want to go any more than you don't want me to. But it's the right thing to do.

She slumps back on the bed. Fine.

Oh, don't be like that, Zeet, he says.

She flaps a hand at him. Go, already.

Zeet, come on.

Go! Jesus, she says.

I don't like leaving when we're fighting.

We're not fighting. You're just leaving.

He sighs. I won't be long.

Oh, don't say that now. You're going all the way to Galileo and then back, and then to work, or didn't you just say that?

I did, he admits.

So you'll be long. But whatever. Go, already.

He finishes putting his shoes on and stands up, tall and lean in the dim light.

I love you, he says.

Fine, she says. Get out.

Poppy sits on the floor outside her compartment, arms resting on the rail, feet swinging over the edge. Six levels up, and her only view is more compartments. If she looks upward, she can only see the sloping roof high above, curving away in the distance. Compartments everywhere.

Galileo feels like a slum to her. That's what residents on the other stations called it, anyway. The slum. It isn't particularly grimy, and the residents care for it as best they could, but they're crammed together like shipping containers on a hillside, and most of the station is a long way from anything that constituted a view of the stars.

Poppy describes it sometimes as life inside an old radio.

And that's sort of how Galileo looks. Like the guts of a very large machine, converted into living spaces.

There's an ever-present white noise here, a low, persistent grinding sound, as if the entire station is a single gear in a larger engine. The surroundings are colorless, like an assembled but unpainted model.

When Zeke arrives, Poppy is sipping synthetic juice from a cup.

Hi, Poppy, he says.

Zeke, she answers.

He stands on the balcony behind her, waiting.

Sit down, she says, patting the floor.

He does.

Not much of a view, is it, she says.

I guess not, he says.

He folds his arms on the rail and lays his head down.

Tired? she asks him.

His eyes are closed, but he nods. Very.

I'm sorry, she says. It's so much of a trip here.

It's alright, he replies.

You should go inside and lie down. Rest up a little.

Zita's waiting for me, he says. I should get to it.

Poppy scoots a little closer. Get to what?

Zeke opens his eyes. Whatever you called me over for, I guess.

Oh, Zeke, she says. You didn't have to come tonight. It wasn't anything urgent.

It didn't sound like it was nothing urgent, he says.

I'm sorry. I didn't mean to give you that impression. It could've waited.

Zeke closes his eyes, then pushes away from the rail and gets to his feet.

Zita's going to kill me, he says.

Well, then don't tell her, Poppy says. Here, come inside. You can lie down awhile. Then you can catch the transport back to Tycho. She doesn't have to know you didn't fix anything.

Zeke scrunches his face up.

You're exhausted, Zeke. I can see.

He exhales slowly. What do I tell her I fixed?

Poppy smiles and takes his hand.

Close your eyes, Poppy whispers.

Zeke is stretched out on the sofa. He's too tall for it. His feet are propped up on one end, and his neck is cramped. He scoots around uncomfortably.

What is it? Poppy asks.

I think your couch is too small for me, he says.

Close your eyes.

I don't know, Poppy. Maybe I should --

Shhh, Poppy says. Let me show you something my mom used to do.

Zeke lies long and still on Poppy's bed. There are toys on the floor around the room. He tripped on one when Poppy pushed him through the doorway.

Where's Olive? Where's Max? he asks.

Ollie's staying at her friend's compartment tonight. Max is on a field trip. Now, shhh.

Zeke stares up at the ceiling. I'm a little uncomfortable with --

Poppy places her palms over Zeke's eyes.

Her skin is smooth and cool against his warm eyes. His eyes close, and he feels a deep breath escape his lips.

There you go, she says. Just breathe.

Her palms rest on his eyes for what feels like several minutes. He has almost drifted into sleep when she gently draws her hands away from his face. The sensation nudges him into a foggy dreamspace, and he opens his eyes. They're heavy, and sink closed again.

Stretch out your fingertips for me, she says. Extend them all the way out. Open your palms.

He does so, slowly.

Good, she says. Now stretch, stretch, stretch your fingers as far as they'll go.

He does.

Good, she says again. Now hold that stretch for as long as you can. And then, when you're ready, try to relax your hands -- but slowly, as slowly as you can do.

Zeke's hands go limp, and he feels tension leaving him. It feels like a wash of cool heat.

Good, good, Poppy says. Now your feet and your toes.

He stretches his feet. He can feel his toes crack.

Poppy flattens her thumbs against Zeke's brow and smooths away the worry lines.

Shhh, she whispers again.

She begins to hum deep inside of her chest, a sweet, quiet melody.

Zeke's eyes are shut, and his consciousness is fading fast.

He barely feels the brush of her hair as it settles on his shoulders. Her breath is warm and smells like wine. He can almost hear her heart beating. His muscles slacken, and he feels as if he is sinking deep into the bed and rising off of it at the same time.

He sleeps.

Zita frowns. It has been hours, more hours than would be needed to fix a broken switch, and Zeke has not come home. She's already checked the transport feeds, but there have been no delays. Zeke should have been on the one that docked two hours ago, but he wasn't.

She dials his band again.

There is no response, her A.I. says.

It's not like him, Zita mutters.

There has been a pattern, says the A.I.

What? Zita asks.

A pattern has emerged.

A pattern of what?

Zeke travels to Galileo three times per month. He has been traveling to Galileo for seven months, for a total of twenty-three visits.

Twenty-three, Zita says. I didn't realize it was so many.

Zeke informs you of Galileo trips approximately eighty-five percent of the time, the A.I. points out.

What is Zeke's status right now?

Zeke's metrics are protected, the A.I. says.

Override.

Overrides require authentication, Zita.

Authenticate, then. Authenticate.

Zeke has a password.

Zita's face goes blank. Why?

Because Zeke established a password.

You have to tell me what his status is, Zita says. What if he's injured somewhere?

If Zeke is injured, I am obligated to inform medical authorities. Zeke is not injured.

When did Zeke give you a password? Zita asks.

June 11, 4:22 a.m., the A.I. replies.

Zita feels her face growing hot. So he's lying to me, she says.

The A.I. is silent.

If he's -- wait. Zita snaps her fingers. Show me the screenview log.

The wall panel illuminates.

June 11, Zita says. Four a.m.

The compartment appears onscreen. It's dark, but Zita can see a tiny dash of light where the washroom is. The door is not closed firmly. Nothing is happening.

Speed it up, Zita says.

After nine minutes, the washroom light goes out, and Zita can see Zeke's shadowy form exit. He walks out of frame, and the image shifts to their sleeping quarters. Zita is there, asleep in bed. Zeke stands over her for a long moment.

Zita shivers.

He lightly drags his fingers down her blanketed form, then leaves the bedroom. The image shifts again, and Zeke is making a cup of tea in the kitchen. He speaks, but Zita can't hear him well.

Transcribe, she says.

The A.I. issues an audible transcript of the dialogue.

Zeke: --- message when she wakes.
A.I.: Yes, sir.
Zeke: What's the transport status?
A.I.: Transports are clear. No delays.
Zeke: Okay. I want to set a password.
A.I.: All-person, or for your person?
Zeke: For my person.
A.I.: What is your desired password?
Zeke:

Hey, Zita says. What happened?

The contents of Zeke's speech are in direct conflict with Zeke's privacy preferences, the A.I. says.

Goddammit, she says. What is it?

I cannot reveal that information, the A.I. says. Please be aware that repeated attempts to secure that information will require that I inform Zeke of this conversation.

Zeke can go straight to hell, for all I care, Zita snaps.

I can? Zeke says. What did I do?

Poppy sits at the rail, staring out at the beige slum.

Her neighbors -- the ones that leave their compartment door open, not the neighbors who never emerge from within theirs -- are listening to the pulse station. The uprising on Argus is all that's on the pulse these days.

Hey, Rosalie, Poppy calls.

Her neighbor leans out of the compartment. Too loud?

No, no, Poppy says. I heard that the insurgents were succeeding. Is that true?

Rosalie shakes her head. I'm not listening. Jakob knows. Jakob!

No, Poppy says. It's fine, it's fine.

But Jakob appears in the door beside Rosalie.

Rosalie says, Poppy wants to know if the -- what did you want to know?

Poppy sighs. I asked if the revolt was --

Oh, man, Jakob says. There's a rumor that the guy leading the revolution, that Gerard guy -- there's a rumor that he's actually descended from the Bogleman clan. They say he's going to overthrow the station and then rebuild the Harvard Club.

Shit, Poppy says. No shit? The Harvard Club?

It's just a rumor, Jakob says. Personally, I think he doesn't know what he's going to do if they win. He seems a little, I don't know, like wet dough. You know?

Wet dough, Poppy says. Sure.

Poppy's wrist vibrates.

Sorry, Jakob, she says, pointing at her wrist.

Jakob nods and waves, and vanishes inside again. Rosalie smiles, then follows, chattering at Jakob.

Poppy touches her wrist, and says, When are you coming back?

There is silence, and then Zita's voice says, He isn't coming back.

Zita, Poppy says.

He isn't coming back, Zita repeats. Tell me you understand.

Listen, Poppy says, but Zita interrupts.

Tell me you understand.

Poppy is quiet.

Zita says, No more repairs. No more broken switches. No more money to float your ass. No more middle-of-the-goddamn-night visits. No more naps in your bed.

He told you about that, did he, Poppy says.

Zeke tells me everything, Zita says.

I bet he doesn't, Poppy says.

Everything.

Did he tell you how it happened? The first time?

You're going to leave him alone, Zita says.

How all I had to do was breathe in his ear, and he was mine?

Shut up, Poppy, Zita says.

Did he ever tell you how much he likes it when you bite his ear? It's like an off switch, he just goes --

Listen and listen good, Zita says. If either of us sees you again, ever, I will break your fingers. I learned that once, in a defense class. It's not hard at all. And if you like that sort of thing, the fingers make this sort of happy popping sound -- just like your name, imagine that -- that just make you want to keep breaking them so you can hear it again and again.

There is an edge in Zita's voice that Poppy has never heard.

She remembers the way Zita defended her once at school. Even then, she didn't sound like this.

Zita, Poppy starts.

The nice thing about fingers, Zita says, is that when they're broken, you realize how helpless you are. How alone. How cut off from everything around you.

Zita, she says again.

If you come near him again, Zita says. That's what I'm going to do.

Zita, listen --

But Zita is gone.

Zita exhales slowly.

Her fingers, flexed like claws, soften.
She feels the adrenaline drain away.
Her eyes are closed.
She measures her breathing, slows each breath.
Then she opens her eyes.
Zeke stands in the door, staring at his wife.
Zita smiles at him.
What do you say? she asks. Shall we go out for breakfast?
And she glides past him, into the closet, to dress.

ELDON

When the window is taken away from him, he cries.

He has been on the block for -- he doesn't know how long. Perhaps years. Perhaps a few very long minutes.

This is how it is on the block: nothing exists.

He only feels the walls of his cell when he bumps into them. His cell is large, and he rarely finds the walls.

All of the cells are large. He is no one special.

His cell is neither warm nor cold.

There is no light.

When his guards feed him, they first lower the oxygen content of his cell. When he passes out, he is fed intravenously.

When he wakes, it as if nothing has happened.

He never sees another person.

His voice is his only company.

His voice scares him.

He has never seen another prisoner.

He cannot see his hands if he holds them up.
Eldon has never been this alone.

The window is small and square. He does not always know
where it is. No light comes through the window.

Inside his cell it is as black as space.

Outside his cell is space.

He is dimly aware that he is imprisoned on a space station.

Space stations rotate.

They orbit.

They orbit around planets.

Now and then he remembers.

Outside, somewhere, is Earth.

He was born on Earth.

When Eldon finds the window, he presses his face against it.

He opens his eyes as wide as he can.

They might as well be closed.

The darkness chews at his skin until the boundaries
between his body and the darkness are erased.

He is the darkness.

The darkness is him.

He blinks at the window, hungry for light.

But there are no stars.

No moon. No Earth.

No sun.

Before the space station turns towards Earth, the window slides closed.

Once, Eldon's hand was pressed to the glass when this happened.

The tiny, heavy window-door trapped his finger, and he cried out. He pulled and pulled at his hand, unable to free it.

Then the light came.

It had been foreign to him, this hard white stripe that opened in the dark.

It was like a needle to his eyes, and he blinked furiously. The afterimage of the light tricked him, and he saw tiny stripes of light peeling open the walls in all directions.

When his eyes adjusted, they were full of tears that spilled down his cheeks.

He stopped pulling at his hand and blinked into the light.

The white stripe resolved into a shape. It was curved, and not white at all, but pale blue.

Eldon had opened his mouth to speak.

Then the window shade had suddenly clapped shut, taking the tip of his finger from him.

He had wept for days.

Not for his finger.

For the light.

The window remained closed for a very long time after that.

When it opened again, Eldon did not notice.

There was no light.

He stumbled across it some time later, and clung to its edges as if it were a raft.

Then it had closed again.

When Eldon sleeps, he floats.

The prison cells are gravity-free, like deprivation chambers.

Once, on Earth, prison took a man away from the world. Stripped him of the things that were his. Claimed ownership of his body, if not his mind.

In space, prison takes a man's mind.

It starts with his senses.

The cells are dark. A man cannot see.

The cells are climate-controlled. When the walls and the air feel the same, a man cannot feel.

The cells are full of heavy, dense air. A man talks, and can barely hear his own voice.

A man cannot smell. He never eats.
His identity erodes.
He becomes a raw nerve, aching for the light.
And the light is kept from him.

When he sleeps, he dreams of light.
He dreams of the Earth, rising in his little window.
The Earth is brilliant. It is blue, and green. It is a jewel.
The Earth sings to him. His bones vibrate with joy.
He stretches out his hands.
The Earth lifts him into its embrace.
Shhh, the Earth says to him.
It's okay now.
Everything is okay.

INSTITUTION

The insurgents would die in isolation, banished by the fleet government for treason. But Onyx was overturned, and monuments were constructed to remember those who fought for equality. Station Meili, the long-rumored thirteenth station, will not continue the Onyx tradition. If the station is even real.

For nearly one hundred fifty years, there is quiet.

The fleet ends communications with Earth. Mankind has come to a fork in its road, and now travels in both directions, each cluster separate from the other.

Man becomes a creature of the stars.

DAVID

There's no sensation of movement. The Earth seems fixed in the sky. No stars are visible. The moon is a speck in the distance.

Tasneem turns away from the window and stretches out on her cot.

These shuttle rides are nice, she says.

They take a very long time, David replies. *But then, I've nothing but time. So do you.*

Tasneem puts her arms behind her head and looks up at the ceiling. The panels there are transparent, but the only thing she can see is darkness.

Sometimes I think that I just want to steer the shuttle off-course a little bit, she says. What sort of supplies does this thing carry?

Not enough for you to go off the reservation, David says.

I guess you're right, she says. Hey, are you nervous?

That's one of the beauties of not having a body, David says. *No*

288

nerves to get ous.

She smiles. They're going to have a lot of questions for you, aren't they.

You don't think they'll be distracted by the new station? People make a very big deal out of things that were built without their knowledge.

Oh, they'll have plenty of years to gasp about Station Meili. Shiny new objects are only shiny and new for so long, though. No, I think they'll be much more interested in you, Tasneem says.

I have a confession to make, David says.

What's that?

I am a little nervous.

Don't be, she says. You're the smartest man in the fleet. And you're the man with the plan.

I feel like I'm forgetting something, though.

Well, she says. It'll come to you.

I just have a strange feeling, he says again.

It'll come to you, she says. You're David Dewbury.

Yeah, he says.

But he is uncertain.

Tasneem has almost drifted into sleep when David speaks.

Tasneem, he says. *Do you ever think of Audra?*

Tasneem doesn't open her eyes. If you would just read my thoughts, you'd know the answer already.

I don't like to invade your privacy that much, he says.

Thank you.

Do you?

Almost every day, Tasneem says. Do you think of Heidi?

I never stop thinking of Heidi.

You and Audra made a lovely daughter, Tasneem says. If there's one thing I ever could have done, I think I would have had a daughter.

Nothing is stopping you, David says.

I'm stopping me.

Did you ever love?

Tasneem hesitates. Once, maybe.

But you never did anything about it?

I watched people distracted by love, she says. I watched my mother wither when she lost it. Maybe I never consciously decided to take a pass on romance, but I did, anyway.

Do you ever regret it? David asks.

Not generally, she says.

But you're immortal, or close to it, David says. *You don't miss companionship through the long, lonely years?*

I have you, Tasneem says.

They're silent. Outside the shuttle the black passes by, always the same.

I sometimes hate Heidi for her choice, David says at last.

I know. She knew that, too.

She was my daughter, David says. *It pains me to outlive her.*

She made her choice, Tasneem says. For her, it was the right one. Soma was banned, so it wasn't like she could preserve her body forever, like we've done.

She could have preserved her mind, though, David says. *Her mind is what mattered. Eventually, we'd have been able to give her a new body. Just like one day I'll --*

He stops.

Do you want a new body, David?

He is silent for a moment. Then he says, *I don't know. This arrangement, yours and mine, serves a great many purposes.*

But when we make the announcement, secrecy is less important, isn't it? Maybe you could work on a way to build a body then.

I don't know.

Tasneem looks outside. I think I can see the station. It's big.

Tasneem, David says.

Tasneem is quiet.

Heidi has been dead for seventy-one years, he says. *Audra has been dead for one hundred thirty-nine years.*

I miss them both, Tasneem says.

I wish I could die, too, David says.

Tasneem nods. But you can't.

But I can't, he agrees. *There are too many things to do. It sounds terrible to say, but --*

But mankind needs you, she finishes.

But mankind needs me. Yes.

Maybe one day they won't, David.

I fear that day is very far away.

Are you tired of being an eternal consciousness?

When I became one, my mind was clean. Pure.

And now?

And now I have lost my loves.

Tasneem wraps her arms around herself and squeezes tightly.

David can feel it. *It's nice, but it's not enough*, he says.

She relaxes her arms. I know.

They fall into silence again and watch Station Meili as it grows in the viewport.

Tasneem says, It's you and me, David. For as long as forever is.

You and me, he says.

But she can almost feel his sadness.

Station Meili looks like something from a horror movie. It's an enormous sphere sliced into a hundred cross-sections. Each segment of the station rotates independently of the others, some at great speeds, some more slowly. The station is the first to be constructed as a complete universe unto itself, and nobody is quite sure how it was built in secret. It's far too large to have stayed secret for long.

And yet for seventy-eight years, its secret was kept.

Tasneem's shuttle is still hours away, but the station looms into view.

Wow, she says. Do you see this?

Well, David says, *not in so many words, but yes, I understand what you're seeing.*

It is absolutely enormous, she says.

The chatter I've seen on the network says that each segment is a perfect capsule of human interest, David says. There's an agricultural segment, a waste management segment, an education segment. The most interesting level to me is the alternate reality deck. I imagine a person could spend their entire life plugged into that system.

An alternate reality deck, Tasneem says. I didn't know those were real.

This one is, he says. *Program the system, let it build a false reality for you, plug in, and enjoy.*

That's going to be an interesting thing for someone to manage, Tasneem says. What else?

Manufacturing level, many city levels, many residential levels, arboretums, gardens. There's an oceanic level. Entire thing is submerged.

Wow, Tasneem says.

There are a few levels that haven't been discussed yet, David says. *I'm very curious about them, but there's not much information available on the network yet.*

And you have no idea how they kept this thing secret all this time?

Well, they didn't, did they, he says. *There were plenty of rumors about it as early as 2198.*

It's really, really big, she says.

Yes, David says. *They say it will be the first station capable of supporting one billion residents.*

It looks like it, Tasneem says. Jesus. One billion.

The station is covered with scattered lights, many of them slowly moving as their respective segments rotate.

How should we do this? Tasneem asks, nose still pressed to the window.

There's a ribbon-cutting ceremony, David says. *We can crash that.*

I don't want to crash anything, she says.

No, I mean diplomatically. Find a journalist, and let the rest handle itself.

I've never asked you how this feels.

How what feels, exactly? David asks.

How does it feel, knowing you've found a new Earth?

David is quiet for a moment.

He says, *I feel like a spirit guide. The ghost of David past, leading mankind into its next stage.*

Tasneem considers this. Like a Sherpa.

Not like --

David, the spirit Sherpa.

More like --

Hi, I'm David. I'll be your spirit Sherpa today. Would you like to hear about our specials? We've got two great options for you: charred Earth, very crispy, very yummy, or, if you prefer, we have juicy fresh Earth, nice and ripe and...

Tasneem trails off.

You're nervous, too, I see.

She nods. Terribly.

Scared?

She indicates the station. Wouldn't you be?

I am, David says. *That feeling of having forgotten something is like an itch I can't scratch.*

Tasneem looks back outside. This thing almost looks like a military vessel, she says.

Military -- how?

Oh, there are all of these outer doors. They're all closed, but they can't all be docks or airlocks, can they? They remind me of torpedo doors on old submarines.

This is going to drive me crazy, David says.

I'm sure you'll remember whatever it is.

I don't know, he says. *This hasn't happened before.*

The Great Hall reminds Tasneem of a palace. A red carpet runs from the oversized ballroom doors to the marble stairs at the far end of the room. Enormous columns are evenly placed throughout the hall, large red sashes draped about them. Men in pale uniforms stand at each door, dark gray bands stretched across their chests. They wear tall boots and stand erect as the guests make their way into the Hall.

It's like we've traveled back in time, Tasneem whispers.

You don't have to whisper, David says. *I can hear you.*

It's like we've traveled back in time, Tasneem thinks.

I heard you the first time.

The room is very crowded. Thousands of dignitaries and guests have come to view Meili. The media has described it as the great steel pearl of the fleet, but now that everybody has arrived, most can see it for what it really is: a home fit for a king.

This place worries me, David says.

Me, too, Tasneem thinks. But I can't figure out why.

It's too much, David says. *This is the sort of thing that is built for a new dynasty, for a new heir, for a conquering king. I have a bad feeling about it.*

Me, too, Tasneem thinks again. Do you think that's what --

A voice interrupts, booming across the Great Hall.

Welcome! it cries, and the crowd's chatter fades away.

Welcome to the Great Hall of Meili, the voice says.

The crowd applauds politely.

He didn't call it Station Meili, David observes. *All stations are formally referred to first by their, well, station.*

Tasneem squints and can barely make out a figure at the dais.

You've each been invited here today to witness not only the beauty of this grand palace, the voice begins.

Palace, David says. *Not the word you want to hear right now. Tasneem, we should go.*

Tasneem turns around.

David, she thinks. The doors. They're closed and guarded.

To be certain, it is a grand palace, the host continues. But you have been invited here on this historic day, each and every one of you, to witness the great rebirth of mankind. As we are no longer bound by Earth, so are we no longer bound by Earth law. We are a new humanity. We are a new race. We are men who fly, who journey. We reach for the stars, and such reach must be accompanied by great power. Think of what Christopher Columbus once accomplished -- would he have done so much without Isabella behind him?

Tasneem, David says. *I can't get into their system.*

The host pauses and absorbs the silence of the room. Then he spreads his arms wide and says, Your fleet government is dissolved. It is the rule of the Council. Each person present tonight, you received a gift at the door. A lockbox. Please retrieve your boxes now.

How did I miss this? David asks. *Tasneem, how did I miss this?*

Tasneem takes a small silver case out of her bag. She had examined it earlier, but had been unable to open it. There are no markings on the object. It is the most nondescript thing she has ever seen.

The host lifts his hand. He is holding something small that Tasneem cannot see.

With great theatrics, he presses a button on the object.

Tasneem feels the box vibrate softly in her hand. The other guests feel the same thing. Some laugh at the sensation.

The host says, Now, please -- open your boxes!

Tasneem presses the lid of the box with her fingertip. It opens, revealing a gray sleeve. She tucks the box away, and studies the sleeve. It also is free of markings.

A woman beside her gasps.

Tasneem glances over, and freezes.

The woman is holding an Onyx card.

I knew that Nathan's revolt would never be the end of this, David says. *I knew turning Argus wouldn't be enough.*

Tasneem shakes the sleeve into her hand, and a small charcoal-colored card falls into her palm.

Fuck, she thinks.

Forty years later, the card still looks the goddamn same, David says. *Turn it over.*

She turns the card over. On the surface is a small rectangle. She presses her thumb to it, and the card comes to life. A photograph of her -- a very old one, before the streak of white had appeared in her hair -- swims into view, followed by:

Tasneem Anjali Kyoh
78925P72771-09188-XOS
H 5'4" W 128
DOB 2075.06.11

SOMA Expiration: N/A

David, she thinks. David, I want to leave now.

Before the crowd can respond, the host raises his voice and says, Ladies, gentlemen, citizens of this great cosmos...

In the dramatic pause, David says -- and Tasneem thinks -- *Oh, shit.*

Allow me to present, the host finishes, the Grand Council, hereby the ruling body of our prized fleet.

There is silence as four men in rich red robes step forward. Each wears a cap and sash of gold.

Tasneem feels as if she has just traveled a thousand years back in time.

She is speechless.

David is not.

Tasneem, he says. *Did we just begin a new dark age?*

The host steps to the dais again. The Grand Council, he says, with a sweep of his arm.

Then he drops to one knee, and dips his head.

Around the Great Hall, at every door, the armed guards stomp in unison. The threatening clatter echoes in the cavernous room, and Tasneem jumps.

All around her, slowly, people begin to sink to one knee.

To the future of our race, cries the host. To the expression of our great dreams. To the glory of the Council! Welcome, new residents of Citadel Meili!

Citadel, David says. *I knew it. They've just declared sovereignty.*

My god, Tasneem thinks. David, I think I've just become a royal prisoner.

We have plans to make, David says.

Tasneem can only nod.

The four robed men bow serenely, and the host gestures at the crowd to rise.

The people obey.

DEAR READER

Thanks very much for spending a couple of bucks -- and, more importantly, your time -- on my book, *The Settlers*. This book is quite special to me. It's my own personal homage to *The Martian Chronicles*, Ray Bradbury's classic novel of man's colonization of the red planet. I read *Chronicles* every year, finding something new to celebrate every time I open the pages, and I genuinely hope you enjoyed my book even a fraction as much.

The Settlers is the first book in a trilogy about mankind's escape from a ruined Earth. The second book, *The Colonists*, continues the story, and is available now. The third book, *The Travelers*, will be available in 2014 (or possibly a little sooner -- I do like to under-promise).

This is a self-published book. This means that I depend greatly on readers to help me find a larger audience. If you enjoyed reading this book, I hope you won't mind taking a small extra step to share it with another reader who you think might enjoy it, too. Here are a few things you can do to spread the word:

- Rate and review the book on Amazon
- Sign up for the mailing list at jasongurley.com
- Follow me on Twitter (twitter.com/jgurley)
- Like my Facebook page (facebook.com/authorjasongurley)
- Check out and share my blog at jasongurley.com

- Read another of my books!

One of the best things about being an independent author is that I'm more accessible to readers than other authors are sometimes able to be. If you bump into me online, say hello. I'd love to hear from you!

Thanks so much for reading!

Jg

ABOUT THE AUTHOR

Jason Gurley is the author of *Greatfall*, *The Man Who Ended the World*, *The Settlers*, *The Colonists* and *Eleanor*. Born in the squelchy bogs of Texas, then raised in the icy caves of Alaska, he relied on his imagination to keep him warm and dry. As a result, he firmly believes that Superman isn't Superman if he's not wearing red undies, and that Darryl Strawberry had the sweetest swing of all time. He may be the only man alive who believes both, and that's okay.

Jason lives in Oregon with his family, and is a creative director in Portland. He can be found online at **jasongurley.com** and **twitter.com/jgurley**, and probably a few dozen other places, if you look hard enough.

CPSIA information can be obtained at www.ICGtesting.com
Printed in the USA
LVOW01s2133120315

430382LV00011B/346/P